Bo es

camp Liverwurst
& the Search for Bigfoot

Jim Badke

Camp Liverwurst and the Search for Bigfoot
by Jim Badke
©2022, James Badke
ISBN 978-1-7777101-2-5

Cover & Author Illustrations: Mike Fehr
Cover Design: Jennifer Bush (www.northernedge.co)

Author Page & Blog: www.jimbadke.ca
Purchasing, Articles & More: www.campleader.ca

Also available from Amazon in Kindle eBook format,
readable on any device with the free Kindle app.

Contact Jim (www.campleader.ca) for bulk orders or if
your organization is interested in translating this book.

Related books by this author, available on Amazon:
- *Camp Liverwurst & the Stray Compass* (2023)
- *The Christian Camp Leader* (2013)

A Note to Cabin Leaders:

This series of middle-school novels is designed so that each can be read aloud to your campers over the course of a week at camp. Every 12-minute chapter will spark conversations about God. Questions and activities are provided at the end of the book to be used as prompts (not a script!) for discussion. Plan on reading two to three chapters per day— for cabin devotions, during wake-up, after a meal or on a break. Campers will likely ask you to read more each day!

"In this mysterious fantasy, Jim crafts a wonderfully imaginative story, helping the reader see the Gospel through the eyes of a camper who is wrestling with difficult questions about God. What a fun story! And what a great read for a counselor with young campers at camp, to help open up meaningful conversations!" – Pat Petkau, ED, Forest Springs Camp & Conference Centre

"Jim Badke has done it again! Camp Liverwurst *is another valuable contribution to the Christian camping community. These adventures at Camp Liverwurst in the lives of the campers and staff will provide the backdrop for many deeper and better-focused cabin conversations that God will use for His purpose and glory."* – Dan Bolin, Director of Christian Camping International (retired)

"Jim has provided an innovative, tangible and creative way to facilitate the important relationship between a camper and their cabin leader, and a camper and God. An excellent resource for cabin leaders to encourage God discussions." – Sharon Fraess, National Director, Christian Camping International - Canada

"Fun. Imaginative. Original. Jim Badke's Camp Liverwurst *brings the world of Bible camp to life in a most unexpected way. Complete with discussion questions, this book will engage your campers' minds and hearts with a story that is sure to create thought-provoking discussions on what it means to be a follower of Jesus."* – Bill McCaskell, National Director, One Hope Canada

"From decades of experience, Jim has created a tool that will help cabin leaders be more effective in guiding meaningful spiritual conversations with their campers. Who doesn't like a good story? And the questions will gently lead campers to explore what it means to follow Jesus. I look forward to getting my hands on copies of Camp Liverwurst for the cabin leaders at the week of middle school camp I direct." – Randy Carter, Camp Speaker, STM Ministries

"The book creatively and imaginatively captures so many of the emotions and thoughts a camper experiences in a typical week of summer camp. The reader is invited into Jayden's faith formation journey, recognizing the role that other campers and counselors play in that process." – Rob Tiessen, ED, Camp Squeah

"A creative, enjoyable, and much-needed addition to camp ministry. I love how Jim weaves solid biblical principles into a fun and intriguing story." – Craig W. Douglas, ED, Timberline Ranch & Author of Pillow Fights & Sleepless Nights

"Young campers will love this story as cabin leaders read it to them during cabin time to stimulate faith-oriented discussions." – Kirk Potter, Retreat Center Director, The Firs (retired)

"A wonderfully crafted story designed to ready one's imagination for the wonder of the Gospel." – Tim Paquette, ED, Sunnybrae Camp

"Here's help to reduce cabin leader stress and create a fun environment for Bible discussions." – Amanda Rubert, Former Head Counselor

"The book is brilliantly written and will be a big aid to camp staff, especially those who are new to cabin leading. Make room in the camp toolbox for this one!" – Katie Brown, Emerging Writer & Aspiring Camp Director

"I look forward to reading this book to my campers, who will be eager to see what the next chapter holds. A great way to spark conversations about Jesus!" – Janelle Ten Have, Cabin Leader, Camp Imadene

--- More reviews at Amazon.com ---

CONTENTS

1. Never Thought I'd Ever

Jayden bounced the lawnmower back into the shed. Done, finally! His dad's yard was as big as a golf course and took forever to cut. He opened the back door yelling, "I'm going to Evan's house!" and peddled out the driveway before his dad found more work for him.

Evan wasn't home. So unfair! Evan's mom saw Jayden's face fall. "Sorry, Jayden. Evan and his dad are buying a sleeping bag for his week at summer camp." Jayden groaned inside. "You remember Evan is going to camp tomorrow, right?"

No, he did not! Of all the rotten luck! All his friends were ditching him. Off to their lakeside cabins or road trips. Pretty soon, Jayden would be the last kid left in town. Evan's mom gave him a popsicle, but it splattered on the driveway after the first bite. Perfect.

When Jayden put away his bike and stepped through the front door, the phone was ringing. It was Evan. "Jayden, where are you right now?"

"Duh. In my house," answered Jayden. "Landline, remember?"

"Yeah, whatever," Evan replied. "Hey, my dad talked to my summer camp and they had a cancelation! They have room for one more camper. And they asked my dad if I had a friend who wanted to go. What do you think?"

"Camp? Like cabins and archery and campfires?" Jayden's heart raced. "Um, I don't know. I'm sure we can't afford..."

"Jayden! Don't worry! It's paid for! You can go for free!"

He had never heard happier words. Summer camp! Jayden thought he would never, ever go to summer camp in his entire life.

"Well?" Evan demanded. "Are you coming?"

"Uh, well, y y y yeah!" Jayden stammered. "I gotta ask my dad, though..."

"So ask! I'm not hanging up until you give me an answer. Go!"

Jayden dropped the phone and ran to his dad's "man-cave." No entry without knocking. Jayden pounded the door.

"Whatttt?" The door flew open and his dad glared at him, bleary-eyed. Jayden must have woken him up. He looked crazy and angry.

"Um, like, Evan called and..." Jayden stopped, discouraged.

"Spit it out, boy! And it better be good!"

Jayden took a deep breath. "Well, Evan's camp has one spot open and I can go for free, if..."

"Camp? Like, summer camp? What's it called? Where?" His dad looked skeptical. "And why is it free?"

Jayden had no idea. But his dad had not said "no" right away. He gave him a hopeful glance and dashed for the phone. He heard his dad following him, grumbling.

"Evan, what's the camp called?" Jayden gasped. "And why's it free? My dad needs to know."

"It's the camp where I always go! You heard me talk about it before—Camp Liverwurst." Jayden remembered thinking it was a weird name for a camp. "And it's free because the family who canceled wants someone to go who otherwise... Well, you know..." Yes, Jayden did know. Someone who could never afford it. Like him.

"Okay, wait a minute..."

As he turned to relay the info, his dad grabbed the phone from him. "Evan, put your dad on the line. I want to talk to him." Nuts. Jayden could only watch as his one chance to go to summer camp went down the toilet. His dad closed the man-cave door behind him.

It stayed closed so long, he was afraid his dad might have fallen asleep. Jayden sat staring at the door, trying to remember what he had heard about Camp Liverwurst. He didn't believe everything Evan told him, which was smart with a guy like Evan. Not that his friend was lying; he simply had a brilliant imagination. Half of what Evan told him about his adventures at Camp Liverwurst couldn't possibly be true.

The door opened and Jayden tried to read the look on his dad's face. His dad shook the phone at him. "You know this is a Bible camp, right?" Jayden shrugged. "You won't come home with a bunch of weird ideas about God, right?" Jayden shook his head. "Promise?" Jayden nodded. His dad sighed. "Okay, you can go."

"Yes!" Jayden leaped up from his chair. He surprised

his dad by running over and hugging him around the middle.

"You're welcome," his dad muttered, raising his arms. "Now, get lost."

Jayden couldn't wait for Evan to return home so they could talk about camp. He had so many questions. What should he bring? How long was the drive? And where was this camp anyway? Finally, he climbed on his bike and rode back and forth on Evan's street until he saw their SUV turn the corner.

Evan gave him a huge high-five. "Excellent! I can't believe I finally get to take you to my camp! You're gonna love it!" They sat in Evan's tree fort and talked all afternoon. Jayden found out that the camp was in the mountains a couple hours away. It was next to a lake that was perfect for tubing and sailing and paddling. They would play the wildest games a person could imagine.

"My dad says I'm not supposed to get any weird ideas about God when I'm at camp," Jayden said. "I'm not sure what he means."

"You won't. Not any weird ideas, anyway. The leaders are... Well, I don't know how to describe them." Evan waved his hands. "Out of this world? Fantastic? Anyway, you have nothing to fear."

"I'm kinda scared," Jayden admitted. "I've never been away from home for more than a night or two. A whole week..."

"...will be awesome!" Evan assured him. "You'll see. Being scared is part of the adventure. I love being scared at Camp Liverwurst! Just you wait."

But waiting was hard. That night, Jayden stared at the glowing stars on his ceiling for a long time. He was more than kinda scared. His excitement about going to camp with Evan was turning into fears of every kind. Evan would be the only person he would know. What if Evan ditched him for his other friends? The lake sounded incredible—except Jayden was not a great swimmer.

Finally, Jayden slept. But in his dreams, enormous popsicles chased him through a dark forest, roaring like lawnmowers.

Jayden woke to his dad pounding on his door. "Get up, dude! They're waiting for you!" Jayden rolled right out of bed and sat dazed on the floor. What? Who's waiting? Then it all came back to him. Camp Liverwurst! He and Evan were going today! He threw the last few items into the duffle, grabbed his dad's old sleeping bag and headed for the door. His dad handed him a granola bar on the way. "Don't puke it up in their car, okay? See you in a week."

Evan's family was so fun. As the car climbed up into the mountains, they sang all the silly camp songs, which they said hadn't changed since Evan's parents were campers. After more than two hours, they turned onto a narrow road that curled up a steep valley with huge trees on either side. The air coming through the windows was cool and fresh and scented with fir needles.

"Almost there!" Evan wriggled with excitement. "See? That's the start of the lake. They say it's hundreds of feet deep." Jayden gulped, imagining himself at the bottom. "The camp is halfway along the lake. I can't wait! Hit the gas, mom!" To Jayden's surprise, she did, whizzing around the corners like she had been there a billion times.

They arrived at a large wooden gate. As they passed through, Jayden caught out of the corner of his eye the name carved at the top. He turned to his friend. "Evan! I thought you said the name of this place was Camp Liverwurst! That's not what the sign says!"

"Oh, right. The name's actually 'Camp Livingwaters.' But nobody calls it that. 'Camp Liverwurst' is its nickname." The parking lot was already half-full of campers. Parents unloaded suitcases and sports gear and sleeping bags.

Two men walked toward their car. As they came near, Jayden thought he had never seen anyone like them. One had long wavy hair, tied back, and wore a T-shirt that read, "How can I help?" The other had a thick beard and bald head, and was dressed like a sailor. Jayden couldn't decide if they were young or old.

As Jayden took this in, he was hugged by the T-shirt guy and thumped on the shoulder by the other one. "Hey, boys," the T-shirt man greeted them, "so glad you're here! I'm Barney and I'll be your assistant cabin leader. Here, Jayden, let me grab your bags."

"And I'm Noah," the other said. Jayden looked up at him and jumped back. Noah had a long, fat snake entwined over his shoulders and down both arms. "Oh, don't mind old Ichabod—he's harmless." The snake stuck out a black tongue at Jayden and hissed. "I'll be your cabin leader this week. Good to see you again,

Evan! Thank you for bringing your friend." He picked up Evan's bags and nodded for them to follow.

Jayden's jaw was still somewhere down by his knees. Evan had to prod him before he started walking. "Incredible! We're so lucky!" Evan exclaimed. "These guys are the best! Never a dull moment with Noah around, and Barney will do anything for us. We've hit the jackpot!"

"The s-s-snake..." Jayden could hardly speak. "Please tell me the snake doesn't stay in the cabin."

Evan snorted. "The snake is nothing! Just you wait!" They followed Barney and Noah through a corridor of massive trees. A wide lake soon sparkled into view.

Evan's parents jogged up behind them. "Wow! I can't believe it! You have Noah!" his dad exclaimed. "And Barnabas! I had Noah as my leader when I was twelve!" Jayden stopped and stared at him. How on earth...? Evan's dad laughed, "You guys will have the week of your lives, and no mistake!"

Jayden whispered to Evan, "How could your dad have had the same cabin leader as us when he was our age? He must be..."

"I'll explain later," Evan replied. "C'mon!" After a short walk through the trees, they arrived at the lake. To Jayden's surprise, he saw no buildings. Instead, a small marina contained boats of every description. There were canoes and kayaks, paddleboards, sailboats large and small, jet skis, wakeboard boats and fishing vessels. He saw a ship the size and shape of a small ferry, towering above the rest.

"Evan, where's the camp? I'm freaking out here. Do

we spend the whole week on boats?" Jayden stared at his worst nightmare.

"Of course not! Camp Liverwurst is on the other side of the lake, at the base of the mountain." Far across the water, Jayden saw jagged peaks and patches of snow that crowned a steep slope of tall green trees. "This way! Noah's boat is the biggest."

That was good news to Jayden. The lake looked a bit rough. Some campers were storing their gear into little compartments in their kayaks. Others were hugging their parents goodbye and putting on lifejackets. Kids and leaders clambered onto fishing boats or hoisted tall white sails on beautiful wooden sloops. The boys crossed a wide flagstone quay and entered the wooden boardwalk where Noah's boat was moored.

Noah's boat was crawling with creatures. Two raccoons watched them from the top of the flagpole. Some kind of tag game ranged all over the upper deck—dogs and cheetahs and a very small rhino. Seagulls and ravens and a massive eagle circled endlessly around the wheelhouse. The deafening buzz of whinnying, trumpeting, meowing, oinking and other animal languages meant that many more were on board. Jayden wondered how he and Evan would fit, let alone the rest of the cabin group.

Evan's parents hugged them both. His mom had tears on her cheek—tears of joy, she assured Evan as he pulled Jayden up the gangplank. Everyone stood at the railing and waved goodbye. The two of them were squeezed uncomfortably between a kangaroo and a baby elephant.

Most of the boats had departed. An old wooden sailboat had already capsized a short distance from the dock. Its cabin leaders were handing their campers various parts of the boat to cling to. Another cabin group appeared to be striding across the water with packs on their backs and some type of floats on their feet.

"No worries," Evan reassured his friend. "This happens every year. We all make it safely across the lake, eventually. It once took Jonah's crew three days! We should arrive in half an hour." Noah's boat pulled away from the dock with a thunderous blast of its horn that made Jayden jump. They were off on a week's adventure, and Jayden knew now that anything could happen.

CAMP LIVERWURST & THE SEARCH FOR BIGFOOT

2. The Best Day Ever

"Welcome aboard!" Noah's voice came loud and clear over the intercom. "This vessel is equipped with every safety feature. In the event that we start going down, flotation devices are stored under every seat, and lifeboats will be deployed." Jayden groaned inside. The wind was strong, and they were already crashing through big waves.

"No need to fear, campers!" Noah assured them. "We managed to keep our assets afloat while the whole world was in liquidation!"

"Huh?" said Jayden.

"Don't worry about it," replied Evan. The boys stepped into the lounge, where an enormous brown bear took up an entire couch, snoring loudly. "Want anything from the boat's store?" Evan asked. "I'm buying."

But Jayden didn't trust his stomach. "No thanks. Can we go back outside?" When they returned to the rail, Jayden faced his friend. "Evan, what on earth is going on? I've never heard of anything like this place. Is it real, or are we both having the same dream?"

"Hey, I know. I felt the same way the first time. But trust me, you're safe here." Evan said this as a skunk sauntered by, raised its tail at them, then changed its mind and carried on. "Camp Liverwurst is... well, different. You won't find any place like it on earth. I could tell you more, but you'll figure it out in a few days. Until then, nothing to fear." The boat lurched sideways and Jayden gripped the railing like his life depended on it.

Other than being sat on by an apologetic moose, the rest of the trip was uneventful. The closer they came to the other side of the lake, the quieter the waves and wind became. Jayden saw a large building made of logs rising out of the trees. Small cabins were scattered along the shoreline on either side. Noah came up behind the two boys and placed his hands on their shoulders. "What do you think, Jayden? Is this the adventure you were expecting?"

"I-I-I'm not great at adventures, sir." The boat swerved wildly. "Um, who's steering the ship right now, if it's not you?"

Noah pulled his beard. "Oh, it could be anyone. We usually let campers navigate their own way across. Want to give it a spin? And by the way, none of that 'sir' business around here. We go by one name each, and mine's Noah."

"Um, thanks, Noah. I'm okay with holding on right here." Noah laughed warmly and walked away.

"Isn't he great?" Evan watched in admiration as Noah entered the wheelhouse. Five minutes later, it seemed the skipper had taken the wheel again. They set a straight course toward a marina identical to the one they had left. Only a few of the boats had arrived before them. Jayden was glad he wasn't stuck halfway across the lake in a swamped canoe.

As they gathered at the gangplank, Jayden met his other cabinmates. Some looked as confident as Evan, who joked with them like they were old buddies. A few others looked as freaked out as Jayden. But he liked the look of the group of guys he would spend a week with. He could imagine them as friends.

"Our cabin is farthest from the Lodge, for the sake of the animals," Evan grunted as he pushed his full wheelbarrow along the dock. "We'll take turns, right?" A wide trail littered with fir cones led them along the shore. The log cabins they passed had unusual names like Mizpah and Jericho and Ramathaimzophim. Jayden looked back once and saw that an entire herd of creatures was following the boys. Great. He wondered how many he would have in his bed, like giant unstuffed toys.

"Here we are!" Jayden helped Evan push the wheelbarrow up the steep path. The name on the cabin was "Mount Ararat." Jayden hoped rats weren't actually welcome inside. At the bottom of the stairs, he turned and looked back. More massive mountains ranged along the other side of the turquoise-blue lake. A boat was lowering its sails as it reached the marina. Jayden felt like he could soak in this view all day.

Barney was sitting on the railing. "Hey, guys! Go ahead and pick a bunk, new campers on the bottom, veterans on top. One less reason for newcomers to be afraid to go to the bathroom in the middle of the night, hey?" Jayden hadn't thought of that—he always needed to get up at night. In the dark? In the woods? Oh boy.

Evan snagged a bunk for them with a view of the lake.

Noah arrived with a koala bear that he transferred to a post before coming inside. "Everyone find a bed? Anthony, no turkey vultures in your bunk, okay? We'll try to keep the critters outside, but hey, you know critters, right? They're a bunch of animals!" He laughed as a llama poked its head through an open window. "Let's gather around the table and get to know one another."

In the next half hour, Jayden found out that Nabil's family had arrived a couple years ago from Syria. He had a limp from an old injury. Michael was into Lego and Logan could burp the entire alphabet backwards. There were ten boys altogether. Alex was from the same city as Evan and Jayden. Liam and Mason were twins, and Christopher didn't know anyone else at camp. The vulture was still on Anthony's shoulder.

"And Jayden! Last but not least. Who lives at your house, Jayden?" Jayden could tell Barney actually wanted to know.

"Only me and my dad." Jayden scrambled to think of fascinating things to tell everyone. He didn't come up with much.

"Pets? No? Big spiders?" Jayden shook his head. "Cool, sounds like a nice tight family." Yah, right, Jayden thought. "Hey, tell us about your best day ever," Barney asked.

Jayden wanted to impress these guys with a great story and it was tempting to make something up. But he couldn't do that to a guy like Barney. No one had taken such an interest in him before. "I guess... I guess, it would be... today." He realized that was true. "I mean, I'm still kinda freaked out, being here and all. But it's been my best day ever."

"Wow," said Noah, "Jayden, that's so encouraging. Thank you!" He looked at Jayden with eyes of appreciation. "And my guess is, each day this week will be even better." He stood up. "Everyone ready? It's time for food and fun! We'll grab lunch here. Then Barney will take you to see what Deborah, our activities director, has planned for this afternoon."

Barney retrieved a platter of fresh sub sandwiches from a cooler. The excited boys could not help wolfing down their lunch. Especially when a real wolf crouched under the table, eating the scraps they slipped him.

As the campers surged out the door after lunch, Jayden asked Evan what they would be doing. "Beats me!" he answered. "But it'll be awesome, whatever it is. They didn't tell us to put on our swimsuits, so we must be doing land activities first." Jayden sighed in relief.

As they followed Barney, the boys met other campers pushing wheelbarrows or carrying backpacks. Some were soaking wet, but laughing and excited just the same. "Evan, where did all the girls go?" All Jayden saw were dudes.

"The girls' cabins are on the other side of the Lodge. That's the big building we passed when we came in," Evan replied. "See? Here come some of them now." They had entered a small clearing and a group of girls approached from the far side. Barney greeted the girls' cabin leaders, Abigail and Mary. But the two groups held back, eyeing one another awkwardly.

A man stepped up with a couple of huge bins in his arms. "Hey, everyone! Welcome to Camp Liverwurst... I mean, Livingwords! Whatever. My name is Jonathan, and Deborah asked me to start you on some activities. You look like two groups who need to get to know one another. How about archery?" It sounded okay to Jayden, but looking around, he didn't see any targets to shoot at.

Jonathan took an archery bow from a bin. "Who has shot an arrow before?" Many of the campers raised their hands, including Evan. Jayden had never touched a bow before. "Great! But have you ever played archery tag?" They all looked at one another and shrugged. "Who wants to be tagged by an arrow?" Jonathan notched the arrow to the bowstring, pulled back and fired.

Everyone gasped and ducked. The campers heard a loud thwack and an "Ouch!" Turning, they saw Barney standing behind them, hand to his shoulder. He was wearing a face mask like the one Jayden wore when they went paintballing on Evan's last birthday. Barney's shirt had a big pink spot that spread out under his hand, and what was that smell? Strawberries? The arrow was lying on the ground.

"Nice shot, Jonathan!" Barney shouted. He bent down and picked up the arrow. "See, it has a soft end instead of a point. Kinda feels like someone hit a ping-pong ball at you quite hard. And when it hits you, scented powder marks the spot to prove you were hit." He sniffed at the spot on his shoulder. "But I need to warn you, not all the arrows smell like strawberries."

The campers started talking excitedly and dove for the bins. "Hang on, hang on," Jonathan laughed. "All in good time. But first, some shooting instructions and a few rules to follow." Ten minutes later, the guys were all at one end of the field, the girls at the other, each of them with a bow in hand. At first, everyone was cautious. A few random arrows flew but didn't hit anyone. They all kept their distance, not wanting to be the first target.

Suddenly, Christopher ran toward the girls, yelling his head off. Before he could shoot, five arrows hit him with puffs of yellow and green and white powder. He dropped his bow and went to his knees, gagging. "No! Not rotten eggs and... cooked cabbage and..." He picked up an arrow. "Hey, popcorn-scented!"

Christopher's casualty got the other guys moving. Skirting around the neutral zone circle where Christopher now had to stay, they started firing at the five girls who had no arrows. Evan tossed stray arrows to his cabinmates so they could fire another round. Soon, three girls had to join Christopher in the circle. But now the other girls had all the arrows! They charged and soon made short work of the remaining guys. All the boys had bright splotches of stinky color on their shirts and masks.

All except Jayden. Terrified, he had stayed back as far as he could, hoping not to be noticed. His one arrow was gone, a wild shot that sailed over everyone's heads into the trees. The three remaining girls approached him, arrows aimed at his chest. It was all over. "Should I get him, Emma?" a tall girl asked grimly.

"Let's all shoot at the same time," another suggested.

"No, we want him to suffer, Maddie! One at a time," the third girl sneered. "You first, Olivia."

Olivia aimed and let loose her arrow from twenty feet away. Jayden wasn't sure what happened next. Eyes wide, he dodged sideways—and grabbed the arrow right out of the air.

"Yes!" he heard Evan yell. "That means you get to go back in the game, Christopher!" Out of the corner of his eye, he saw Christopher dive out of the neutral zone and grab a spent arrow. Jayden kept his focus on the girls who were still facing him. The second one took her shot, and the other right after her. Flinging his bow and arrow to the ground, he snagged their arrows out of the air with each hand.

Four guys were on the field now, including Jayden. It was pandemonium for several minutes. Arrows flew, girls screamed, guys yelled and every imaginable smell was in the air. Jayden grabbed two more arrows as they flew by him, and soon the boys had won. Jayden was the only one without splotches of color on his clothing.

"Awesome, Jayden!" The guys crowded around him. "Have you played this before?" "I couldn't believe how you did that!" Jayden couldn't believe it either. His head swam with all the praise poured on him. It seemed that grabbing arrows from the air was like second nature to him, but he had no idea how.

He didn't have the chance to get a swelled head about it. The girls were quick at picking up strategies. In the end, the guys won two rounds and the girls three. Everyone raved about the game as they left the field together. Maddie and her friend Olivia asked Jayden to teach them his skill of arrow-snatching.

Jayden had never felt better about himself.

3. Absent Without Leave

The afternoon flew by like an arrow, and soon a big bell in front of the Lodge sounded for dinner. Jayden, Evan and Alex sat at a table with their competitors, Emma, Olivia and Maddie. Barney joined them and introduced his friend Solomon, the camp caretaker.

The buzz of excited conversation faded as a man stepped up to the microphone. "Welcome to Camp Liverwurst!" he bellowed. Everyone cheered and yelled and clapped their hands. "My name is Peter—thank the Lord—and I'm your host this evening. Are you as hungry as I am?" Campers shouted "yes" and "no" and "I'm hungrier!"

Peter lifted his face and his hands toward the ceiling. The room went silent and Jayden realized that Peter was praying. "Our Father in heaven, " he began, "your name is like no other on earth. Thank you for sending each of these young men and women. We love each one, just as they are. And I pray we will love them too much to leave them just as they are. For the abundant food we are about to eat, we are grateful. We pray in the name of our beloved boss, Jesus the Messiah."

Jayden never forgot his first dinner at Camp Liverwurst. At home, meals were in front of the TV, often by himself, and rarely lasted to the first commercials. Here, dinner was as much about talking as eating. Emma and her friends told Solomon all about archery tag that afternoon.

"Tell me about your best shot," asked Solomon. Everyone one-upped each other about their archery skills until it became ridiculous. "But Jayden was the best," said Maddie, "grabbing arrows right out of the air like that. You were amazing, Jayden!" Jayden's face turned red.

"Did any of you have shots that missed?" Solomon asked. Of course. Everyone missed most of the time. Even Jayden wasn't able to snag every arrow that went by. "We all miss the mark, don't we, whether in archery or in life," Solomon said, looking around the table. "We all mess up sometimes." Jayden agreed. He was an expert at messing up. That's what his dad always told him.

"Here's my question for you: What's the mark you're missing?" Solomon asked. "You knew your target when you were shooting arrows at one another. But what are you aiming for in life? What's the target you so often miss?"

Many things came to mind. Olivia said her school marks were never good enough for her parents. Alex talked about a video game he could never beat. Finally, Evan spoke up and said, "I guess you want us to say that our target is God, right? But I don't like that idea."

"Why not, Evan?" Solomon asked quietly.

"Well, it's not fair! Why should anyone expect me to be as good as God? Like, I try hard, most of the time. But there's no way I'm as perfect as God."

"You're exactly right, Evan. Neither was I." Jayden thought there was something weird about the way Solomon said this.

"There you go," Evan replied. "It's not fair."

"Evan, are you sure you have a clear view of your target? Do you know what God expects of you?" Solomon and Evan stared at one another. "You're too smart for me to hand you the answer, Evan. I'll give you some time to wrestle with the question."

They sat silently for a while. Campers at the other tables started leaving the dining hall. Solomon broke into their thoughts. "Let me say this, that once you are sure of your target, missing it is the only thing to fear in life. Nothing else." What? Jayden didn't get it. He could think of many things to be afraid of.

Solomon pushed his chair back. "Wonderful to meet all of you! I know I'll remember our conversation!"

As he left the table, Barney said, "That's one wise dude! Think about what he said." He stretched and stood. "Okay, then, who's ready for a nature hike?" Silent stares all around. Jayden was up for anything, except swimming without a life jacket. But a nature hike didn't sound as amazing as archery tag.

"Wow, not much enthusiasm! You're coming too, girls," he called after the three as they started to walk away. "Gather up your group and meet us on the front steps in ten minutes, okay?" The girls rolled their eyes and walked off toward their cabin.

As they left to get ready for the hike, Jayden thought about Solomon's words. "Evan, what did Solomon mean when he said, 'Neither was I'? Like he was talking about himself in the past."

Evan stopped and turned to Jayden. "You don't get it, do you?"

"Get what?" Jayden replied.

Evan sighed. "It's not your fault. You didn't grow up going to church like me." They started walking again. "The names of all the leaders here—do they sound familiar?"

"Kinda. Some are weird. I've never heard of anybody besides a dinosaur named 'Barney' before."

"It's short for Barnabas. And you met Noah, Peter, Abigail, Mary, Jonathan and Solomon. You'll meet many more. They all have names from the Bible. Do you know why?"

"Because it's a Bible camp?"

"Yeah, but there's more to it than that," Evan replied. "The leaders here don't just have Bible names. They *are* the people from the Bible."

Jayden smirked. "You mean, they're pretending to be the characters in the Bible stories. Acting like them. Right?"

"Nope! That's not what I mean." The lights of the cabin appeared in front of them. "They're not acting. They're the real people." Jayden's stomach did a twist. He went silent as they walked through the door.

"Everyone here?" asked Barney. "Right! Grab a warm hoody and a sturdy pair of shoes. See you on the front steps in five minutes."

On the way back to the Lodge, Jayden walked with

Noah. "What's on your mind this evening, Jayden?" Noah asked.

Jayden took a moment to answer. "Evan told me... Well, he said you and the other leaders were... are characters... um, people from the Bible. He can't be right, can he? He's only joking. You're all acting, right?"

"It's hard to believe, isn't it?" Noah replied. "I have trouble believing it myself sometimes. But Jayden, it's true. I really am Noah, the guy who built the ark." They passed a woman who was leading a small herd of sheep along the path. "Hey, Rachel!" he greeted her. To Jayden, he said, "That's the wife of Jacob, the father of the twelve tribes of Israel. We're the real thing!"

"But... but how could that be?" Jayden stammered. "I thought people in the Bible lived thousands of years ago. How can you be here, and now?"

"A good question, Jayden." He put his hand on Jayden's shoulder. "I don't have an answer for you. All I know is, each summer we find ourselves at Camp Liverwurst. You and these other wonderful campers show up, and we have a fantastic time together!" Seeing Jayden's anxious look, he added, "If you want some advice, do what I do. Don't worry about it. And soak up every minute!"

Since worry was one of the things Jayden was best at, he found Noah's advice hard to take. When they arrived at the front steps, the guys were talking about the big game coming up later in the week. If it was anything like the past games they were describing, Jayden wasn't sure he wanted to play.

Evan was laughing, "One time, I reached for a flag

31

hanging in a tree. A motion-detector sprinkler went off, spraying maple syrup!" He looked around at the guys. "By the time I made it back to our base, I had so many leaves and twigs stuck to me, no one could tell who I was!"

"It was an improvement, actually," said a voice behind him. Emma, Olivia and Maddie had come up behind them and were listening without Evan knowing. "You guys are going to be toast in the games this summer," Olivia sneered. "We'll make souvlaki out of you."

"I don't even know what that is, Olivia," Evan retorted. "But it sounds tasty. Bring it on!" The guys laughed and the three girls glared.

"Alright, then," Barney broke in. "If you're all finished calling out one another like a couple of gladiators, let's go exploring!"

The nature hike started out more fun than they expected. Noah led the way, and Barney, Abigail and Mary kept everyone talking and laughing. Noah pointed out wildlife in places they never would have noticed. A family of foxes peered over some rocks, and several deer stood motionless among the dimly-lit trees. A huffy old badger grumbled across the path when they stopped to watch him.

"How long have you and Evan been friends?" Maddie asked Jayden as they waited by the lakeshore for the stragglers. The sunset reflected yellow and orange on the water.

Jayden wasn't used to girls paying any attention to him, and he was a bit tongue-tied. "Um, uh, as long as

I can remember, I guess."

"How come he's never brought you to camp before?" Maddie asked. She had the longest eyelashes Jayden had ever seen.

He gulped, "Well, somebody paid for me to come. My dad couldn't…"

"Me too!" Maddie interrupted excitedly. "My family could never afford camp. Do you know who paid for you?"

"Nope." Jayden felt relieved that Maddie was like him.

"Me neither," said Maddie. "Every year, I find a note in my mailbox reminding me to register for camp, and every year it's paid for. I don't know who does this, but I wish I knew how to thank them!" Jayden agreed. He hadn't even thought about the person who let him come in their place.

They left the lakeshore and joined the other campers, who were crowded around some thorny bushes. "What on earth did that come from, Noah?" Christopher's voice was shaky.

Noah pulled a clump of hair from the bush, held it to his nose and sniffed. It was long and coarse, a mix of brown and gray. Noah sighed. "Skookum, what are you up to?"

"Who's Skookum?" Olivia asked.

Noah stuffed the hair into a pack he carried over his shoulder. "Skookum is a friend of mine," he answered lightly.

"Human friend or animal friend?" someone

shouted. When everyone stopped laughing, Noah chuckled, "Yes, that's the question, isn't it?" and continued down the path with no explanation. The group followed, quieter than before.

"What did he mean by that?" Jayden whispered nervously to Maddie. "Why wouldn't he know if his friend is human or not?" Maddie didn't answer. Jayden continued, "I don't think Noah is always very safe to be around..."

The group had stopped again. They stood by a small stream that flowed into the lake. Everyone was staring silently at a patch of muddy ground. Jayden and Maddie pushed through the crowd to see what was up.

In the mud were two footprints. The prints were barefoot and pressed deep into the ground. And they were twice as big as any human footprint Jayden had ever seen.

"Those aren't bear tracks," stammered Evan. "I don't see any claw marks."

"Besides, that would be one giant of a bear," Emma added.

Everyone turned and looked at Noah, who held up his hands and said, "Okay, okay! I'll tell you. These footprints are further evidence that my friend Skookum has gone AWOL: 'Absent-Without-Leave.'"

"Is your friend a hairy giant that walks around with nothing on?" asked Olivia.

Everyone laughed, including Noah. "You guessed it, Olivia!" he chuckled. The campers all went silent again. "You might find this hard to believe. My friend

Skookum is a Bigfoot. The Bigfoot, actually. A Sasquatch. He might be the last of his kind. I'm rather fond of him." Everyone stared at Noah, mouths open in shock.

"W-w-what do you mean, he's gone AWOL?" Everyone looked to see who had asked the question. It was Jayden. His face was drained of color.

"Skookum lives in a cave on the mountain." Noah sighed and rubbed his bald head. "I taught him to stay up there because people panic when a Sasquatch shows up. It appears he's left the mountain for some reason. I guess we need to go and find him."

After a moment's silence, the whole group burst out at once. "Go and find him?" "Is he serious?" "Those tracks are fresh!" "Let's get out of here!" And, "Mommy!!!"

Jayden felt like he might pass out. He and Evan once watched a video about hunting for Sasquatches. He didn't sleep for a week after that, and wouldn't even take the garbage out after dark. According to Noah, nothing but trees and air were between him and a real, live Bigfoot somewhere ahead. And Noah wanted to track it down!

4. A Good Kind of Fear

To Jayden's great relief, Noah decided not to look for Skookum the Sasquatch right away. "It will be dark soon," he explained. "I'll talk with Nehemiah, the camp director, and see what he thinks we should do. For now, please don't talk about this and panic the other campers."

As they continued their nature hike, the campers paid little attention to the trees and bugs and rock formations the leaders pointed out. Everyone was listening for sounds in the woods around them. They saw no more sign of Skookum, but he was always on their minds.

As they arrived back at the Lodge, a bell rang out right above their heads. Jayden jumped a foot off the ground. "What's that for?"

"Chapel!! One of my favorite times of day!" Evan led Jayden around to the front of the building. Streams of campers climbed the stairs to a big room above the dining hall. Big fluffy cushions were scattered all over the wooden floor, but no one sat down. A woman and a guy with a guitar started singing and a whole band joined them—drums, bass, lead guitar and a violin—while everyone sang and danced. Jayden thought the band sounded pretty good. The words to the song were projected onto the wall above the dark windows.

He is my rock ("rock, rock," everyone shouted)
and the God who rescues me
He is like a fortress to me
so I will always be okay
I depend on God to rescue me
and make things okay
He is my mighty rock ("rock, rock")
and my place of safety
Trust in him at all times
Everyone
Tell him all your troubles
God is our safe place

Jayden thought about what he had promised his dad: no weird ideas about God! What would his dad think of this? Was God like a rock and a fortress? Could God be trusted? Jayden mouthed the words but didn't sing them because he wasn't sure if they were right. His friends around him were singing themselves hoarse.

Everyone yelled and cheered at the end of the song. As Peter took the microphone, they collapsed down on the cushions. "Wow, great start to chapel, Miriam and David!" he thanked the singers. "You can keep going in a minute. Right now, Moses is coming up to remind us of some guidelines we all need to follow this week so everyone has the time of their lives. Moses?"

Peter handed the mic to an older man dressed in yellow pants, yellow shirt, yellow hat and polka dot tie. He looked so much like an elderly version of Curious

George's owner, Jayden almost expected a monkey to climb up into his arms. The man put on some thick spectacles, cleared his throat and began to read from a long piece of paper. The camp had rules like the boys staying out of the girl's cabin area, and keeping off the dock when it was closed.

Then he stopped and grumbled something under his breath. He stuffed his glasses into his shirt pocket, crumpled up the paper and tossed it over his shoulder. "Enough of that!" he exclaimed. "Really, all we ask is that we love one another. Can we do that?" Everyone cheered and pounded their feet on the floor. "What I mean by love is, notice the needs of the people around you. Think about how you would want to be treated if you were in their shoes. Consider how kind and patient God has been with me and you, and let's do the same for one another!" He smiled broadly at them. "Have a wonderful week!"

Everyone got to their feet as the music started up again, a wild song that made you want to dance. Miriam started a conga-line, each person with their hands on the shoulders of the person in front of them. The line wound through the crowd, getting longer all the time. Jayden didn't join in, but the music made his body move and sway—though not his feet, which were glued to the floor.

"That was so fun," Evan gasped as the song came to an end and everyone sat down. "You should've joined the line! Your dancing reminds me of the inflatable tube guy at the car dealership." Jayden laughed and pushed Evan off his cushion. The room became quiet as Peter introduced a man named Stephen, who spoke with a quiet, confident voice that made Jayden want to listen.

"Everyone, take a deep breath!" Stephen sniffed loudly. "Smell that?" Along with the scent of sweaty bodies, Jayden detected something delicious. "I'm guessing chocolate chip cookies for our snack tonight. Anyone hungry?" Everybody was! When the room was quiet again, Stephen continued, "Can you imagine never being hungry again? Maybe that sounds good, but if you were never hungry, you might forget to eat and even starve to death.

"Who didn't find a cushion to sit on? You, young man, is your bottom getting a bit sore? Hey, someone, toss this guy a cushion!" Dozens of cushions sailed through the air until the poor guy was buried. "Can you imagine never, ever being in pain? Yes, that sounds good. Except you wouldn't notice when you hurt yourself or your appendix was about to burst. You wouldn't stay healthy very long without pain.

"Who came to the camp dock in a car or truck? How did the driver manage to steer all the way here without crashing into something? I'll tell you—it was fear. Can you imagine drivers having zero sense of fear? Driving through red lights? Ignoring the lines on the road? None of you would have arrived here. There is a kind of hungry that is good and a kind of pain that is essential. In the same way, there is a kind of fear that makes people better drivers."

Jayden knew lots about fear, but he had never thought of fear as a good thing. He listened to Stephen intently. "There is, of course, a bad kind of hungry, a nasty kind of pain, and a terrible kind of fear," Stephen continued. "These are not things we would wish on anyone, though they're unavoidable. You would never become a good driver if you were too afraid to get behind the wheel of a car. Or imagine if I was terrified of God. I wouldn't be standing up here telling you about him. I might never get out of bed!

"But I'm not terrified of God. I love him and I trust him. At the same time, I also fear him. How does that work? Martha, please bring up the plate of cookies I asked for." The incredible scent of fresh chocolate chip cookies wafted past Jayden and Evan as the camp cook brought a huge tray up to the front. "Thank you, Martha! Okay, I need a volunteer." Everyone's hand shot up and pumped the air.

To Jayden's great surprise, Stephen chose him! "Yes, you, Jayden. Come on up." His cabin group watched with envy as Stephen held out the cookies to him. "Now, I bet you thought you were volunteering to eat a cookie. Actually, Jayden, you volunteered *not* to eat a cookie! But you can hand these out to everyone else. Be sure not to eat any yourself, okay?" Everyone laughed as Stephen handed the tray to Jayden.

As he served out the cookies, Jayden fumed inside. He had been tricked! Why should everyone else have a cookie and not him? The scent of the cookies right in front of his nose drove his senses wild. He thought about sneaking one into his pocket, but everyone would see. In moments, not a cookie was left.

"Thank you, Jayden, for not eating a cookie," Stephen said as he took the tray back. "I know you wanted to, and you had only two reasons not to eat one. First, because you would get caught by everyone, and second, because I said so. Which one of these two reasons was yours?"

Jayden gulped. It was like Stephen could read his mind. "It was because I would get caught," he admitted sheepishly in front of the whole crowd.

"I appreciate your honesty," Stephen replied. "There was one other reason for you to not eat a cookie, a reason I knew and you didn't. Jayden, these cookies were made with real vanilla." Jayden's face went white. "What would have happened, Jayden, if you had eaten one of those cookies?"

Jayden stammered, "I... I... would have... broken out in hives."

Stephen looked straight into his eyes. "I know, Jayden. I checked the medical form your dad sent in. You're the only one here this week who is allergic to real vanilla. Eating it gives you itchy spots all over, sometimes for days. That sure would have messed up your week at camp!" Jayden felt weak and went to sit down with his cabin, but Stephen called after him. "Jayden, next time I ask you not to eat something, what will be your reason for not eating it?"

Jayden turned. "Um, because you said so."

"Because you're scared of me?"

Jayden thought for a second before answering. "No, I'm not scared of you. I'm scared now of doing something you tell me not to. Because you know things I don't, and... I trust you."

"There you go, Jayden," Stephen replied kindly. "You learned a good kind of fear today." Jayden sat down with his friends. "If we all learned to fear God this way, we would find ourselves in a lot less trouble," Stephen continued. "He knows things we don't know, and we can trust him because he loves us perfectly. Solomon, our caretaker, once wrote that the fear of God is the beginning of wisdom. It's the place to start if you want to make better decisions in any situation in life."

Stephen talked for a few minutes longer. Jayden's thoughts wandered to the many times he had been so afraid, so freaked out about everything. He remembered Solomon's discussion at the table about having only one thing to fear. What if this was it? If he could learn to fear God and nothing else, it might change everything.

Evan had to shake him out of his thoughts and drag him downstairs to the dining room. Everyone was enjoying cookies and hot chocolate before they went back to their cabins for the night. On the boys' table was a big plate of chocolate chip cookies with a little paper flag on top that read, "No vanilla."

When they arrived back at the cabin, Noah was sitting on the steps, scratching the ears of a mountain lion that rumbled contentedly beside him. "Don't come too close," he warned them. "If I wasn't around, this cat would do what any wild animal does. He's not a tame lion."

The cougar purred and nudged Noah's arm to get him scratching his ears again. "I saw you boys sneaking tidbits to the wolf under the table yesterday. Remember that to a wolf, young boys' fingers are also food, a delicacy really. No feeding the animals! Human food gives them gas. Take that whichever way you like." As if to underline his words, the mountain lion jumped down, licked Anthony's face and smacked its lips. The rest of the boys shuffled several feet away. Noah chuckled as the cougar wove its way between them and out of sight.

"Come inside, everyone!" said Noah. "Our first day has been a full one, and we have another tomorrow." Everyone got ready for bed. Barney had them all crowd onto his bunk and he read them a chapter from a book. Jayden found the story interesting—all about a land where the animals could talk and the king was a lion—but he just… couldn't keep… his eyes… open…

"Jayden!" He heard Barney's low voice like he was far away. He opened his eyes. The cabin was dark and the sounds of sleeping campers were all around. Barney had his hand over a flashlight so it wasn't too bright. "Hey, I traded bunks with you, since you were already asleep in mine. I'm heading to the washroom, and I thought you might need to as well."

Jayden nodded and followed Barney in a daze. As

44

they reached the washroom, he saw the lights of the marina reflecting softly on the lake. They made the shadows seem all the blacker. He was so glad for Barney because he couldn't imagine being out in the dark alone. Then he remembered that a Bigfoot was wandering somewhere in these woods, and he shivered.

CAMP LIVERWURST & THE SEARCH FOR BIGFOOT

5. Fingerprints All Over It

The next morning, as the campers devoured their waffles and scrambled eggs, Deborah the activities director got up to make announcements. After breakfast, the campers could choose any one of the many activities the camp offered. Jayden and Evan ran straight to the BMX biking shed and had a great time riding the tracks that ran through the forest. They rode bumps and drops, and Jayden tried out the smaller jumps.

They took a break on a wooden deck overlooking the lake. Jayden leaped up as the bushes below them began to move. Oh no, he panicked. Bigfoot! He was about to jump onto his bike and ride away when a man emerged from the trees by the lake. He was tall and muscular, and he wore camouflage clothing and a backpack. The man looked like he had just walked off the screen of an action movie.

He looked surprised to see the boys. "Hello, there!" he called up to them cheerfully. "Mind if I come up and join you?" Not waiting for an answer, he climbed up onto the deck in one motion. Jayden and Evan just stood there, gawking at the huge rifle the man wore over his shoulder.

He held out his hand. "Flintlock's the name. Doctor

Robert Flintlock." He took Jayden's hand in a grip so tight, Jayden couldn't grip back. He could feel his cheeks flapping as Dr. Flintlock shook Jayden's entire body.

Evan held back his hand and scowled at the man. "What are you doing here?" he asked him accusingly. "And what's with the rifle? Don't you know this is a summer camp?"

Dr. Flintlock didn't seem to notice Evan's tone of voice. "Actually, I was about to ask what *you* are doing here, out in the woods by yourselves. Isn't it time you headed back to the Lodge? We were starting to worry about you."

Jayden breathed a sigh of relief. "So you're one of the camp staff?"

"Of course," the doctor replied. "Why else would I be here?" He took the gun off his shoulder. "See? Take a look." He opened the gun's magazine and showed them a row of large colorful darts. "I keep an eye out for straying camp animals—Noah's bunch—always wandering out of bounds. These darts help me bring them back safely."

Evan stood, arms crossed and looking unconvinced. "Noah's our cabin leader, and I can't imagine he needs someone like you watching out for his animals."

"Well, he can't be everywhere at once, can he? Which is a good reason for you to go back now and check in with him." When Evan didn't move, the doctor said impatiently, "Off you go, before they have to send out someone to look for you." He waved them onto their bikes. "And no good using me as an excuse for being back late. Not many of the staff members know about me. I work incognito." The boys rode off as he watched them.

Evan was riding super hard; Jayden couldn't keep up. He saw out of the corner of his eye that Evan had taken a side trail, and he made the turn just in time. His friend had already put his bike away when Jayden arrived at the shed. "Evan, what on earth?" he yelled as Evan strode away toward the Lodge. Jayden rode after him. "What's going on? Who was that guy, and what does 'incognito' mean?"

Evan grabbed Jayden's handlebars. "'Incognito' means he doesn't want anyone to know what he's doing. And as for who he is, one thing's for sure—he's not one of the camp staff!" He started jogging across the field.

"Wait!" Jayden called after him. "How do you know he's not one of the camp staff?"

Evan yelled over his shoulder, "Last time I checked, no one in the Bible was named Robert!" Jayden's heart sank. He put away the bike and ran toward the Lodge.

It took Evan and Jayden half an hour to find Noah, who was doing some work on his boat. When he saw the boys, he gave them each a can of stinky creamy stuff and a rag. He showed them how to rub it on all the brass fittings and polish them until they could see their reflection in the metal.

As the boys interrupted one another's story about Dr. Robert Flintlock, Noah's eyes narrowed. "Yes, I've met the person you describe. And no, he's not assisting me. Quite the opposite." Jayden concentrated on polishing the ship's bell, which helped him calm down.

Every time he thought he was finished, he found another fingerprint on its glossy surface.

"Dr. Flintlock has visited before," Noah continued. "He was full of questions, most of which I didn't want to answer. He has a... um... unhealthy interest in our friend Skookum the Sasquatch."

"He had a gun!" Jayden's words shocked Noah. "Well, a dart gun, but it was huge." Noah relaxed, but the boys could tell he was still concerned. He had them describe exactly where the boys had last seen the doctor.

"The Doctor is a far better woodsman than me," Noah said. "He won't want to be found, and he has many ways of hiding." Noah took Jayden's rag and showed him how to do one section of the bell at a time until the whole thing gleamed. "Dr. Flintlock isn't the only one hiding, is he, Jayden? We're all good at hiding, especially from God."

Jayden gulped. Was God searching for him? The thought that God might be looking for him troubled Jayden. Maybe if he knew he could trust him, it would be okay if God found him. Jayden worked up his courage and asked, "Noah, what's God like?"

Noah's smile was as bright as the brass bell. "What is he like? Look around you, Jayden! Listen carefully! Breathe deep! Soak it all in!" Jayden walked to the railing and leaned against it. He stared at the deep green of the water and the whiteness of the few puffy clouds against a brilliant blue sky. Jayden listened to the cries of seagulls and the laughter of a cabin group putting their canoes away. A slight breeze ruffled his hair and brought him the scent of bread baking at the

Lodge.

He turned and asked Noah, "You mean God is like... like nature?"

Noah shook his head. "No, no, he is much greater than that. But Jayden, nature is like God. You can see his fingerprints everywhere on what he created. They are far more numerous than campers' fingerprints on the ship's bell. The world tells you so much about God, day after day. That he's beautiful and awesome, that he's gentle and terrifying, that he's wise and good."

Evan left the railing he was polishing and joined their conversation. "What about natural disasters, like earthquakes and hurricanes? What do those tell us about God?" Evan's tone was doubtful.

"The natural world also tells us about ourselves," Noah replied. "It reminds us that we're small and fragile. We live in a broken world. I couldn't count the times that I had to call on Someone to rescue me."

"You mean like a SAR team?" Jayden asked excitedly. "Those guys are so cool, saving people with helicopters and hanging down cliffs."

Noah laughed. "Yes, sometimes we could use a good Search and Rescue team. But we can't call 9-1-1 every time something bad happens. God allows us to go through hard times so we will learn to call on him for help. We're reminded of how much we need him."

Jayden wasn't sure about this. Like, he had lived his whole life without God. Why would he need him now? He remembered his promise to his dad. It was time to change the subject. "So, Noah, aren't you concerned about Dr. Flintlock?"

"I am curious about his gun," Noah admitted. "But no, I'm sure Skookum is even better at hiding than the Doctor."

"Is that what the wide game is about tonight?" asked Evan. "Finding Skookum?"

Noah laughed again. "I hope there's more to the game than that, or everyone's in for a big disappointment. I don't know all the details, but I was told to wear full camouflage. I'm sure Esther and her team have something scrumptious planned for tonight's game." Noah collected up the brass polishing stuff and thanked them for their help.

"Why is it called a 'wide game'?" Jayden asked Evan as they walked off the dock.

"It's called a wide game because we use the whole camp to play," he explained. "Sometimes we have to go out and find things that are hidden. Or carry an object from one place to another without getting caught."

"Caught by who?" Wide games were starting to sound pretty creepy to Jayden.

"The bad guys!" When Evan saw the look on Jayden's face, he assured him, "Don't worry. The bad guys are actually the good guys. Like, they're all our leaders. Sometimes they dress up in costumes, and they chase us around the woods to make the game more challenging. But the worst they'll do if they catch you is make you sing the 'Baby Shark' song."

"That's bad enough!" Jayden shuddered. "Do you really think we'll look for the Sasquatch? What happens if we find him?"

"I don't know," Evan laughed. "Maybe we win!"

Or lose, thought Jayden.

The boys went to the camp store where the feature of the day was fresh huckleberry ice cream. They sat on a bench on the dock and watched a group of campers learn how to roll their kayaks in the water. They each came up spluttering. It was pretty funny to watch. "What do you think this doctor guy wants with Skookum?" Jayden asked between licks of his cone. "Like, what's with the darts in his gun?"

"I guess it's a tranquilizer gun," answered Evan. "But that doesn't make any sense. If he knocks out Skookum, what will he do with him? Drag him away? He couldn't move a creature as huge as Skookum must be."

They sat and thought about this in silence until their cones were gone. As they stood up to leave, Emma, Olivia and Maddie and the rest of their cabin group blocked the boys' way. "So, did you think that was funny, Evan?" Emma looked furious.

Evan looked stunned for a moment, then frowned and crossed his arms. "Well, if you're going to blame me for something, at least tell me what I did so I can enjoy it!"

The girls glared at him. "How did you guys do it?" Maddie shouted. "That took a lot of nerve—hanging all our bunks from branches in the trees!"

"Whaaat?" Jayden shouted back, standing beside his friend. "You're crazy! No way could we do that! And why do you think it was us?"

Olivia held out a book to Evan. "Recognize this?

Maybe you should read it more, instead of leaving it at the scene of the crime."

Evan took the book, which was a Bible with his name on the front in bold graffiti letters. Inside, the Bible was full of colored notes he had written in the margins. "Where did you find this?" he demanded.

"On the floor in the middle of our cabin," said Emma accusingly. "I should say, on the bare floor of our cabin! Thanks a lot for leaving all our suitcases and pillows in a pile in front of the door."

Evan leafed through the Bible, thinking hard. Who would have done this? He looked up at the girls and said in a quiet voice, "I don't know what's going on, but I lost this Bible when I was at camp two summers ago."

"Yeah, right," scoffed Olivia. "What was it doing in our cabin?"

"Well, remember last summer, when they decided to switch the guys' and girls' cabin areas? I think your cabin was my cabin two summers ago."

The girls had no answer to this. Finally, Maddie broke the uncomfortable silence. "So, you didn't empty all the stuff out of our cabin?" Evan shook his head. "Then who did?" All the girls started talking at once. Evan and Jayden looked at one another and shrugged.

As they walked away past the group of girls, Emma shouted after them, "Hey, aren't you going to help us?"

Evan turned. "Help you what?"

"Get our bunks out of the trees and find out who did this?"

Evan made a mock show of pondering the question

and said, "Hmmm... Nope!" and walked away.

Jayden jogged to catch up to him. "Evan, that was kinda rude and really awesome at the same time!" Evan kept walking and didn't seem to notice what Jayden had said. "Evan?"

Evan put his hand on Jayden's shoulder as they kept moving. "Jayden, have you noticed how heavy our bunks are? Like, do you think you could lift even one end off the ground?" Now that Evan mentioned it, Jayden remembered that the bunks were made of small logs all fitted together and had big, thick mattresses. They must weigh a ton.

"Yeah, like who on earth could pick them up and hang them in a tree?" Fear crept up Jayden's neck like cold water. "We couldn't do it if our whole cabin helped us!"

They walked for a few moments in silence. Evan stopped and looked at his friend. "Are you thinking what I'm thinking?"

"Skookum!!" they shouted together. Without another word, they ran off to find Noah again.

6. Take That!

When they told Noah about the girls' cabin and their hanging bunk beds, Noah laughed and then sighed. "I guess we can't put off finding Skookum much longer. He's as gentle as a capybara but about as smart as a bucket. I'm not sure what he was doing in my old cabin—trying to catch a mouse?—but he probably thought he was helping me. I'll send someone to assist the girls."

Later that afternoon, the bell at the Lodge called the boys away from their game of Gaga ball. Everyone gathered on the big stone patio by the front steps. An attractive lady with a clipboard stood on the stairs with a few other staff, who handed a large, shiny coin to each camper. "Hey, everyone! I'm Esther, if you haven't met me yet..." Everyone started chanting, "Quee-nie! Queenie! Quee-nie!" She laughed. "Yep, Queenie will do. Are you ready for the Big Game?" Everyone yelled their heads off.

"Okay, here's how it goes," she continued when they could hear her again. "You may have noticed that most of your camp leaders have disappeared in the last half an hour. Let me tell you what happened. Camp Liverwurst has been infested by Time Parasites. You heard me right! Creatures that feed on time. What gobbles up your time at home?" Campers shouted out things like video games, cute puppy videos and math homework.

"Yes, those can be Time Parasites too," Esther continued. "These ones have attacked your cabin leaders and sucked the time right out of them. Now your leaders are in the woods, frozen in time! What's more, they have been disguised. Your leaders could be dressed up as anything that doesn't move around on its own—from boulders to washing machines. Your assignment? Go find them!" There was a sudden bustle as everyone tried to move at the same time.

Esther stopped them. "Hold on, everyone! Before you go, I have a few more things to tell you. The only way to unfreeze the cabin leaders is to stand around them and sing to them! You can sing any song, but the happier, wilder and louder your song, the faster they will unfreeze."

Campers rushed again to begin the search. "Wait!" Esther shouted. When the campers stopped, she continued. "When you find and unfreeze your cabin leaders, they have something very important to give you: your dinner! But what happens if you unfreeze someone who isn't your cabin leader? That's not so good. Anyone that you unfreeze who isn't your cabin leader becomes one of the bad guys to you—and you know what that means!"

A few campers screamed out a horrible rendition of the 'Baby Shark' song. "Yep, some form of penalty." Esther laughed. "Plus, they will take your coins, which means more points for their cabin and less for yours.

Those cabin leaders will freeze again until their own cabin finds them. You will have to come back here and receive a new coin from me before you can keep playing the game."

"A couple more things!" she yelled, as a few campers tried to make a dash for it. "First, the Time Parasites are still out there. If they tag you, you have to freeze right where you are until your whole cabin group stands in a circle around you and sings 'Baby Shark' – with the actions!" All the campers groaned. "But if you manage to form a circle around a Time Parasite and sing the whole song, it will pop!" Everyone cheered.

"Second, here are some boundaries for the game. If your toes are in the lake..." The campers yelled, You've gone too far! "If you start going up the mountain..." You've gone too far, they screamed. "And if you enter any building..." You're in big trouble! "Right!" Esther concluded. "Now, get out there and find your frozen cabin leaders!"

Pandemonium ensued, but only for a few moments as everyone scurried away. Jayden was about to run, but Evan grabbed his arm and stopped him. "Come in, guys..." Evan yelled to the others in his cabin group—and then stopped. Emma, Olivia and Maddie's cabin had the same idea and were gathering nearby on the patio.

They heard Esther laughing on the steps. "Great minds think alike!" she called. "May the wisest cabin win!" The campers glared at one another. Then each cabin group huddled close together so they couldn't be overheard as they made their plans to win this game.

Minutes later, Evan and his cabin group were dashing through the trees from one big bush to another, crouching behind each one. All around, they could hear muffled calls and singing and cabin groups running by. Several times, they had to flee from Time Parasites—leaders dressed as enormous squeaky toys—who tagged people by bouncing into them.

Soon it was almost dark and they still had not found Noah and Barney, their cabin leaders. They had to get new coins when they unfroze a couple of girls' cabin leaders who were disguised as two giant beach balls. Logan and Anthony reported every two minutes how hungry they were. Jayden agreed. He didn't complain, but his stomach growled noisily and Evan turned to hush him. I can't help it, Jayden's shrug said in return.

Evan gathered his cabin group. "Does everyone know exactly where we are? Can you find this place again?" The guys murmured their agreement, including Jayden who didn't have a clue where he was. "Right!" Evan whispered. "We'll split up in twos and look for Noah and Barney. But everyone comes back here after 15 minutes. Got it?"

Evan divided the group and sent them off in different directions, taking Jayden with him. They hadn't run fifty steps when Jayden caught his foot on a tree root and sprawled face-first in the dirt. The fall knocked the wind out of him, but even worse, he couldn't open his eyes. "Got dirt and stuff... in my eyes..." he wheezed as Evan helped him up. "Can't see... Man, it hurts."

Evan didn't hesitate. "Come on, I'll take you to the

camp doctor!" He took Jayden by the arm and led him as Jayden stumbled along blindly. "It's not far to the first-aid post. Don't try to open your eyes. You'll be okay." He aimed for the one small light in the dark forest.

"Evan, I'm sorry!" Jayden gasped. "I'm taking you away from the game..."

"Don't be ridiculous!" Evan snorted. "It's just a game. Well, and dinner. The doc will fix you up in no time."

They went up a couple of steps and Jayden heard Evan say, "Dr. Luke! My friend fell and got something in his eyes. Can you help him?"

"Of course, Evan!" said a calm, confident voice. "What's your name, young man?" He led Jayden to a chair, where Jayden stammered out who he was and what had happened. "Whoa, sounds like a major wipeout!" Dr. Luke exclaimed. "It must have been awesome! Let's get you cleaned up. Eyes first." He washed the dirt off Jayden's face with a warm sponge.

Evan's voice said, "Hey Jayden, you're in good hands. I'll tell our cabin what happened and then come back." Jayden heard the door close behind him.

"Okay, I'll start rinsing your eyes with saline," Dr. Luke continued, "and you go ahead and open them when you feel ready." The cool liquid was such a relief to his burning eyelids, he soon found he could open his eyes. The doctor was a blur on the other side of a mini-waterfall. After a long while, the doctor stopped rinsing and said, "Blink a few times and tell me if we washed it all out."

Jayden blinked. The doctor smiled and handed him a towel. "That's so much better!" Jayden said. "Wow, thanks. I felt like I'd never open my eyes again."

"That would be sad," Dr. Luke replied. "The gift of sight is a miracle. No wonder the Boss loves to make blind people see again."

"What do you mean?" Jayden was confused. He handed the towel back to the doctor, who was tall and wore a long white coat.

"Ah, that's right," Dr. Luke smiled. "You're new here, correct? Our Boss's name is Jesus the Messiah. Have you heard of him?"

"Well, I guess," he replied. Uh-oh, Jayden thought, more stuff about God. "Why do you call him 'the Boss'?"

"Because that is who he is. Jesus is the one in charge, the leader, the king! And not only of this camp—he came to take over the whole world."

"But he's dead!" Jayden argued. "The cross thing, you know..." He pictured in his mind the cross hanging on the wall of his uncle's living room. The cross always made him feel uncomfortable, especially the man with his arms stretched out on it. His dad scowled every time he saw it.

"You're right, Jayden. Jesus' death would be a big obstacle to taking over the world, except for one thing: his death was part of the plan!" Dr. Luke exclaimed.

"I don't get it!" Jayden muttered. There were many things he didn't get about this place. He stood up and started brushing the fir needles and dirt off his clothes, then stopped. He didn't want to mess up Dr. Luke's office.

"It's okay, Jayden," Dr. Luke reassured him. "I can clean up later. Here, try this." He handed Jayden a lint roller with sticky paper on it. Jayden rolled it over his clothes and soon most of the junk was all over the roller instead of him. "Hmm..." the doctor mused, watching him. "I believe you just discovered a good picture of what Jesus did on the cross."

"Huh?" said Jayden, looking up from his work.

"Jesus is like the lint roller. You had stuff all over you, and now it's all over the roller, right?" Jayden nodded. "We all do bad things, like being mean or selfish, or telling lies," Dr. Luke continued. "Those bad things don't simply disappear. They cling to us more and more until our consciences are covered with them. Do you ever feel that way?"

Do I ever! Jayden thought, and nodded. He was always messing up. Sometimes he felt so bad about himself, he could hardly stand it.

The doctor nodded too. "When Jesus was on the cross, he took everyone's bad stuff and put it all on himself. Much more effective than fir needles on a lint roller. Then he died with that terrible weight of badness on him, and it all died with him. Gone. Forever." Jayden was surprised to see tears in the doctor's eyes.

"But that's not the end of the story!" Dr. Luke burst out, as he paced around. "I mean, we were all so disappointed! We thought Jesus would become the king, and now he was dead. And then... and then... the rumors started."

63

"What rumors?" Jayden was getting interested.

"It all began with some of the women who knew Jesus. They said that they went to his grave, which was like a cave with a big stone in front of it. The stone was gone and the cave was empty!" Dr. Luke danced with excitement around the little office. "At first they were upset that someone had done this. One of the women stayed at the tomb by herself, crying. And suddenly, there was Jesus. Alive again! And later, many other people saw him and talked with him."

"How could that be?" Jayden asked.

Dr. Luke stopped dancing. "What's the one thing people fear the most? Death, right?" Jayden nodded. The biggest fear of all. Dr. Luke laughed, "Death itself was in for a big surprise when it took on Jesus, because Jesus won that fight!" He jabbed his fists at the air. "Take that, death, you old enemy! You are defeated! Not only by Jesus, but by everyone who believes in him." He looked straight into Jayden's eyes and said, "Jayden, you have nothing left to fear."

At that moment, Evan returned. Finding his friend all cleaned up, he dragged him right back into the game. It cost them quite a few coins, but the cabin group eventually found Noah and Barney. They were disguised as two enormous Christmas trees. The campers feasted on a huge taco salad while they told Barney and Noah about the game.

That evening, all the campers and leaders sat around a big campfire by the lake. Sparks flew up red and gold and disappeared among the bright stars above them. David and Miriam and the band led them in singing silly songs and sad songs and lively ones. Then the leaders began to tell stories that Jayden had never heard before—about giants and battles, journeys and shipwrecks—as well as the story about Jesus that Dr. Luke had just told him.

That night, Jayden lay awake in his bunk for a long time, wondering. Was all this stuff about God true? Whether it was or not, Jayden decided he wanted it to be true. Nothing to fear, ever again. He wanted that more than anything in the world.

7. Time to Take Action

Jayden didn't know that a time called 6:00 in the morning even existed. He groaned as Evan nudged him awake for the third time. "Come on, Jayden!" he urged his friend. "Grab your swimsuit! It'll be awesome!" His eyes were still hardly open as he followed his quiet and sleepy cabinmates out the door.

It wasn't until they reached the dock that it hit him. Swimsuit! This meant they were going in the lake! Arggghh! Jayden's idea of awesome was a nice hot tub. Not a cold lake that was a gajillion feet deep. So much for never fearing again! When Barney handed them flotation vests, Jayden was so relieved he could have hugged him. They all piled into a boat that was a whole lot smaller than Noah's. It was a ski boat, with several kinds of boards strapped to its tower.

As they were about to pull away from the dock, a massive black dog leaped into the boat. He almost knocked several boys over the side. Noah laughed, "Hey, at least we got away with only one animal on board! Meet Murphie the Newfie! Newfoundland dogs are natural lifeguards, and we can use his weight." Murphie was sitting on Jayden's feet. Yep, he was heavy!

The boat roared to life and surged through the perfectly calm water. The sun hadn't yet reached the lake, but flooded the mountains all around them. The boys were warm only because they were packed into the boat like sardines, with Murphie in the middle. Out in the center of the lake, Noah slowed the boat and let it drift. "Do we have any wakesurfers with us? Has anyone tried this before?"

No one had any experience with wakesurfing, so Barney jumped into the lake to show them how. He took with him a small surfboard and the handle of a short rope attached to the back of the boat. Noah started the boat off slowly. Barney popped up out of the water on his board, riding the large wave created by the wake of the boat. As soon as he had his balance, Barney tossed the handle to the campers and rode the wave all on his own.

"Wow! Awesome, Barney! How do you do that?" The boys cheered their leader on. Barney rode up and down the wave, jumped the board up in the air, did half a backflip and landed with a huge splash. Noah stopped the boat and returned to where Barney was whooping and laughing.

"Who's next?" Barney yelled. "Jayden! Come and join me in the water!" Jayden's cheers caught in his throat. Before he knew what was happening, the boys had crowd-surfed him over their heads. They tossed him into the water beside Barney, and he came up spluttering and flailing.

Barney took Jayden's flotation vest in a firm grip and helped him calm down. "Okay, Jayden, here we go. Getting up on the surfboard is a whole lot easier than it looks. You got this!" When the boat pulled forward,

Jayden gripped the handle of the rope and felt himself rise up out of the water. But then he panicked. Board and Jayden went flying in opposite directions.

When he came to the surface, he heard his cabinmates yelling. "Nice, Jayden! You almost did it! Try again!"

Barney swam over to him. "That was great, Jayden! Let's give it another go. What do you think went wrong?"

"Um, I pulled with my arms," Jayden gasped, "Like you told me not to." He moved back into position, lying back with his feet up on the board.

"That's right! It is such a human thing to do, to try and pull ourselves up when we have a great big boat to do all the pulling for us." He looked squarely into Jayden's eyes. "I know you'll make it this time." He held Jayden's shoulders and yelled, "Hit it!"

Jayden heard the roar of the boat, felt the water surge around him, and suddenly he was standing up! His board rushed down the green mountain of water toward the boat. Jayden tossed the handle to the guys. For thirty glorious seconds, he rode the wave totally free of the boat, up and down. Then he couldn't keep up, and the boat pulled away from him.

As the boat turned to retrieve them, Jayden heard his new friends going wild. Murphie the Newfie took a flying leap off the boat and swam toward him. All Jayden could think was, I want to try that again. But it was time to give the other guys a chance. Michael and Alex had more trouble than Jayden did. Liam and Mason tried riding the board together, which almost worked. Nabil stayed up so long, the guys had to make him laugh before he would finally fall.

"Breakfast time!" Noah called out. He and Barney stowed the boards away while the boys chatted excitedly about their best rides and biggest flops. Jayden sat back contently, fears of the miles of water beneath him melting away. Breakfast? It felt like they had already spent the whole day on the lake. But the day was only getting started. Little did he know it would be the longest day of his life.

BANG! The boys all jumped at the noise of a gunshot in the direction of the mountain. The echo boomed repeatedly all down the valley. In the silence that followed, Jayden heard a wailing howl, long and drawn out, and much louder than any dog. The sound was unlike anything he had ever heard before. Its eerie echoes died away down the lake. The boys all stared at one another with wide eyes. Skookum! Dr. Flintlock!

Noah started the engine and gunned the boat toward shore with a grim look. When they got to the dock, he told Barney to take them to breakfast. "Don't worry, guys!" he said. "I'm sure Skookum is okay. But no one is to go into the woods without me. Got it?" All the boys murmured their agreement.

All except Evan, Jayden noticed.

Jayden told the girls sitting at their table about the gunshot they heard. "I don't think it's right that they haven't done something about that Bigfoot by now," Emma complained. "It's not safe! Why can't they find him?"

Evan hesitated a moment and said, "That's what me

and Jayden are going to do. Find him."

"Are you serious?" Olivia's eyes were wide. "You're going to search for the Bigfoot on your own? Does Noah know?"

"Of course not!" Evan whispered back fiercely. "He doesn't think he needs us. But he's wrong! He can't be everywhere, you know." Jayden was surprised at Evan's plan. It didn't sound right, but he didn't know what to say.

Just then, they realized that the dining hall had emptied. When they arrived upstairs with the rest of the campers, the band was already playing some energetic music. Everyone sat down as the song ended. Since no one went to the front to say anything, the campers began talking among themselves. But soon, one by one, every person went silent as they realized what was happening above them.

No one had noticed the narrow strip of webbing that ran from one side of the room to the other, about 20 feet above their heads. The whole crowd gasped as a woman with long, dark hair and colorful clothing stepped out onto the webbing.

She walked the length of the slackline from one wall to the other with grace and confidence. She walked out again, backward this time, then sat down in the middle of the line and stood up again. The campers gasped in amazement as—in one fluid motion—she did a complete somersault in the air and landed with her feet on the slackline. And then they went wild.

Next, the woman set a small wheelbarrow on the slackline and easily walked across with it. She pushed it one way, then turned around and pulled it the other. She called down to the excited crowd of campers, "Who believes I can push someone across in my wheelbarrow?" Everyone screamed their confidence that she could do it.

She called, "Young lady in the purple T-shirt, come on up and let's give it a try!" The campers went silent and stared at the only person in the crowd who was wearing a purple T-shirt. It was Maddie.

Everyone held their breath. Maddie's face went white, and she stammered, "M-m-m-me? You want me to... to climb into the wheelbarrow?"

"Well, sure!" the woman answered. "I saw you yelling with the rest, and I'm pretty sure I heard you say, 'You can do it!'"

Maddie slowly got to her feet, took one step toward the ladder, and sat down again. "Um, I'm okay. Let someone else go."

The woman nodded. "Thanks for taking the first step, my friend. Alright, how about you with the Vancouver Canucks hat?" A boy not far from Jayden took off his hat and shook his head. "No worries! Let's see... the girl with the bright blue hair—you seem brave! How about joining me up here? No? That's okay!

"But hey," she continued. "I'm pretty sure a few minutes ago, all of you said you believed I could do this! Is anyone ready to follow through with what you said?" She laughed, "How can I know if you believe in me if you're not willing to climb into my wheel-barrow?"

Slowly, awkwardly, one of Jayden's cabinmates stood. It was Nabil. He limped over to the ladder. A couple of the staff steadied him as he made his way up to where the woman stood with the wheelbarrow ready. The room went silent. She held his hand in a firm grasp as he climbed into the wheelbarrow. They went across the line without a waver, back again and then once again. It wasn't until the two of them had climbed back down the ladder that the whole room erupted in screams and cheering and applause.

When it died down, the woman spoke with her hands on Nabil's shoulders. "Nabil, would you like to introduce me to your friends?"

He looked up at her, then at the campers. "Uh, this is my mom. And she's awesome!" Again, the crowd went wild with enthusiasm. They obviously thought both of them were awesome.

When the campers calmed down, Nabil's mom continued. "I have a question for all of you. When I asked if you believed I could take someone across in my wheelbarrow, everyone in this room seemed to say they believed. Here is my question: Of everyone in this room, who really believed in me?"

The campers answered quietly, thoughtfully. Their answers echoed one another around the room. "Nabil... Nabil... It was Nabil... Nabil believed." As he listened, Nabil had a huge smile on his face.

"How do you know?" she asked.

A camper in the front put up her hand. "Because Nabil was the only one who climbed into your wheelbarrow."

Nabil's mom waited until it was completely quiet again. "Pretty obvious, isn't it? Nabil knows me, and he knows I have walked the slackline many, many times. He doesn't just *say* he believes in me; he showed this to be true by climbing the ladder and getting in the wheelbarrow."

She paused, looking at the campers as if she knew and liked each one of them. "I am sure that many of you would say you believe in Jesus," continued Nabil's mom. "But no one—not even you—will know if it's true until your faith is seen in action."

Nabil's mom told stories of their life in Syria during the war, how they stayed and helped their neighbors, even those who were their enemies. They did this because of their faith in Jesus, who said to love people even if they won't love you back.

All the campers were very quiet when she finished speaking. But as they walked down the stairs to go to their activities, a buzz of voices broke out about what they had just seen.

After chapel, Noah and Barney took the boys to a canoe rescue lesson, which was more fun than they expected. After learning how to get a capsized canoe upright again, the boys played a game against Olivia, Maddie and Emma's group. They had to try to dump over the other cabin group's canoes. If a canoe capsized, the rest of their cabin group had to quickly rescue their friends. Emma found a sneaky way of twisting the front of the boy's canoes until every one of them was in the water. Including Noah and Barney!

The next competition was to be the first group to

build a pyramid with their canoes while still on the water. They crisscrossed pairs of canoes on top of each other like a log cabin. There was a great deal of shouting and splashing as each team tried to work out how to do it. Their leaders watched, laughing. Each group should have finished with one canoe on top. That's when they realized that two canoes were missing. Olivia and Maddie, Jayden and Evan—and their canoes—were nowhere to be seen.

8. The Big Difference

The two canoes kept as close to the shore as possible. Maddie, Olivia, Evan and Jayden had to duck under the branches that hung over the lake. Evan held his paddle in the water to stop and the girls pulled up beside them. "We're in so much trouble for doing this!" Olivia wailed. She and Maddie looked scared.

"Serves you right for following us," retorted Evan. "We didn't ask you to, you know!"

"Well, we were curious," said Maddie. "We figured you were off to find Skookum and we didn't want to be left out." She flicked water from her paddle in Jayden's face and he almost fell out of his canoe in surprise. "What's your plan, anyway? Do you think we'll find Skookum by the lake?"

"Nope," replied Evan. "But if we can find Dr. Flintlock's boat, we can find Dr. Flintlock." By way of explanation, Evan jabbed his thumb over his shoulder at Murphie. The Newfoundland dog took up the entire middle of the canoe and threatened to capsize them every time he moved. "Come on! If you want to follow us, you have to keep up."

"You're on!" Olivia glared at him. Their paddling turned into a race, water flying everywhere. Jayden tried desperately to keep them from zigzagging. The girls laughed triumphantly as they pulled ahead of the boys.

"No fair!" shouted Evan. "Murphie's weight slows us down!" Paddling as hard as they could, the two boys could not keep up with the girl's canoe.

Suddenly, Jayden yelled, "Stop!!" and jammed his paddle in the water to slow them down. Out of the corner of his eye, Jayden had seen a narrow opening with overhanging trees and a flash of white that could be a boat. He quickly turned the canoe around to investigate.

"What's up, Jayden?" Evan asked his friend. "Where are you taking us?"

Jayden looked back to see that the girls had turned around too. "I saw something. Maybe it's the doctor's boat." They entered a creek that tugged gently at their canoe, making it hard to keep a straight course. The water was deep and emerald green. They had to lift branches to make their way at first. Then the creek opened out to an oval pool with a waterfall pouring into the far end. Near the waterfall, a white dinghy with an outboard motor rested on the gravel shore.

"Good job, Jayden!" called Maddie as they crossed the pool. Jayden's heart gave a skip at her words. Since when was he good at things? Ever since arriving at Camp Liverwurst, it seemed! He beached the canoe softly right beside the dinghy and Evan clambered out to pull their canoe up. The girls landed moments later. Maddie smiled up at Jayden. "I guess you win!"

They inspected what must be the doctor's boat, but it contained only a cooler, a tank of gas and a fishing rod. Evan picked up the fishing rod and held the handle to Murphie's nose. "Take a good sniff, Murphie! We need you to lead us to Dr. Flintlock." The dog snuffled loudly a few times while covering the handle with drool. Then he backed off and began sniffing around him. Suddenly, Murphie woofed and bolted up a steep, narrow trail beside the waterfall. The campers scrambled to keep up.

The trail soon disappeared. Murphie was weaving everywhere through the ferns and between massive trees. "Why is he doing that?" Olivia exclaimed.

"He's searching out the scent," said Jayden excitedly. "I saw this on TV. Each of his nostrils smells things separately so he can tell which way a scent is coming from." Murphie stopped for a moment, nose wiggling, then barked and started up a steep slope. At the top, a sunny rock rose above the trees and gave them a view of the lake below. Murphie turned around three times, sprawled out on a thick carpet of moss and promptly went to sleep.

"Great! Now what?" said Maddie as they sat down around the dog. To Jayden, the camp dock below them seemed far away. He was amazed at the distance they had come in search of the doctor.

"We wait, of course!" Evan replied. "Murphie probably needs a little break." The dog growled in his sleep, rolled over and began snoring loudly.

"What a day!" said Jayden. "It feels like we went wakesurfing yesterday, but it was only this morning." The boys told Maddie and Olivia about the fun of riding the wave behind the boat. Then they talked about Nabil's mom and how brave he was to join her on the slackline.

"When she invited me to go up, my heart stopped," said Maddie. "I don't mind hiking up a hill like this, but I don't like heights."

Evan snorted, "She *would* have to turn it into a Jesus thing, though. I guess that's what we get for going to a Bible camp."

"What's wrong with that?" Maddie replied. "I liked her stories! They helped me understand what it means to believe." Jayden agreed but didn't say anything.

"Well, I like the people at camp and all, but why does everything have to be about Jesus?" Evan complained.

Maddie looked at him for a moment before answering. "Can I tell you something? When I first came to this camp, I didn't know anything about Jesus or the Bible. But I watched people like Abigail and Peter and the rest, and I realized they had something I didn't have. Now I know what it is. Their faith in Jesus makes them who they are."

Evan focused on busting a small stick all to bits. He looked uncomfortable, but Maddie continued. "The problem is that you feel like you *have* to believe because it's what you grew up with. And you're not sure if you want to. I didn't get that chance, but now I *want* to believe in Jesus. And that's a big difference."

No one said anything for a minute. Then Jayden spoke up. "I want to believe in Jesus too. But I'm scared to trust anyone like that. Trusting people... it hasn't gone so well for me in the past." He tossed a small rock into the trees to stop the tears that tried to form in his eyes. "Trusting Jesus might be as hard as climbing into Nabil's mom's wheelbarrow."

"I think so too," said Olivia softly.

Murphie started snuffling loudly. Eyes still closed, the dog waved his nose around, sniffing everywhere. Suddenly, he leaped up, knocking over Evan and Olivia. The dog turned a circle and dashed into the woods. The campers scrambled up to follow him. Murphie was already out of sight, barking madly.

Now they were pushing their way through thick undergrowth in a small valley. When they finally caught up with him, Murphie was running up and down in a space where the bushes had been crushed and broken. Something enormous had pushed its way through them. As they approached, Evan caught a glimpse of a shiny thing on the forest floor and reached down to pick it up. It was a cartridge from a rifle.

"I bet this is where the gunshot we heard came from," exclaimed Evan.

"Yeah, and we know what he hit!" Jayden said. "Come on! We need to find Skookum and see if he's okay!" He started to follow the path of broken bushes. After a few moments, he realized no one was following him. "Hey!" he called back, "Aren't you coming?"

Maddie, Evan and Olivia looked at one another. Olivia replied, "Um, a creature that's big enough to clear an opening through those bushes? I would rather not find it, thanks!"

"Evan?" Jayden looked at his friend.

Evan shook his head. "I don't get it," he answered. "You're usually the one who's scared of everything! How come you want to track down a Sasquatch in the bush, and we're the ones who are afraid?"

Jayden had to wonder about that for a moment. Evan was right—what on earth was he thinking? But something unfamiliar stirred inside him, and he knew what he had to do. "Well, I'm going whether you come or not. Skookum must be hurt, or he wouldn't have wailed like that. And I'm going to make sure he's okay."

The other three watched as Jayden turned and struggled on toward Murphie's distant barks. Evan, Maddie and Olivia shrugged at one another and followed. They thrashed their way past broken bushes. A branch scraped across Evan's shoulder, and when he looked, he was amazed to see something dark red on his sleeve. Had he cut himself?

"Hey, Jayden, wait!" Evan saw Jayden stop and look back. "Check this out—it's blood, but it's not mine. It must have rubbed off on my shirt from the leaves." He pushed forward to show Jayden. "You were right— Skookum is hurt!"

They hurried on again as fast as they could, which wasn't very fast. Murphie's barks sounded closer and more frantic. They soon caught up with him. Murphie was barking and growling at a large log that lay across their path. Maddie went down on her knees and peered under the log to see what the dog was upset about.

After a moment, she stood and—with a look of disgust on her face—held out something bright blue. "Gross! Look at this. What on earth is it?" They crowded around to look at a metal cylinder with an orange cap. A thick, barbed needle extended from the cap and was covered in a mess of blood and coarse brown hair.

"I don't get it," said Evan, looking closely at the tip. "This definitely looks like one of the darts Dr. Flintlock showed us. But if it's a tranquilizer dart, how come Skookum didn't fall down?" Looking ahead, they could see that the path of crushed bushes kept going up the mountain. "And why is it so covered in hair and...?" He was about to say more, but he didn't want to upset the others. Wherever this dart hit Skookum, it must have left a hole in him.

Just then, the campers heard a whoosh of giant wings above their heads. A massive eagle dropped from the sky and perched on a boulder right next to them. They didn't dare to even breathe. The eagle lifted one wicked-looking set of yellow talons and dropped a small roll of paper to the ground. The bird waited until Olivia picked up the roll, then lifted into the air and flew away.

"That was awesome!" breathed Jayden.

"What does it say?" demanded everyone as they tried to look over Olivia's shoulder. She read the paper out to them: "Follow Murphie back to camp. Now! And walk carefully—no injuries on the way down! - Noah."

"Busted," groaned Evan. "Now what do we do?"

"We do what Noah told us, of course!" replied Maddie. "Anyway, I don't think we'll find Skookum this way. Plus, we need to show Noah the dart."

"And face up to what we've done," said Jayden. "I don't think Noah is happy with us." Jayden was relieved to be going back to camp. He wanted to help Skookum, but the more he thought about it, the less ready he was to meet a Bigfoot in person.

Evan called, "Here, Murphie!" The big dog rushed up and almost knocked him over. "Good boy. Take us to Noah!" Without hesitation, Murphie pushed his way through the bushes. Jayden was concerned that the dog was not taking them back to the canoes, but he seemed to know where he was going.

Murphie kept stopping and barking at them to catch up. After half an hour, they came to a path that Jayden and Evan recognized at once. "The BMX track!" they shouted together. The four of them ran along the trail, trying to keep up with the dog. In less time than Jayden would have expected, they found the side trail that took them to the bike shed.

Panting, the four campers walked the short distance to the Lodge. They found Noah on the front steps, having a tug-of-war with Murphie over a chew toy. He smiled as they slowly climbed the steps. "Welcome back, adventurers!" he said wryly. "I appreciate your bravery, but to obey would have been better than sacrifice." To Murphie he said, "Thanks for looking after them, old boy!"

They all mumbled their apologies, but Noah waved them off. "That's all fine and good, but I'll let Nehemiah handle the discipline side of things." He pushed Murphie off his lap and gave his attention to the campers. "What I want to know is, what did you find up there?"

Evan handed him the blue dart, and Noah examined it carefully. "I'm sure you're right, Evan," he agreed. "This doesn't seem to be a tranquilizer. It looks more as if the doctor was trying to collect a sample."

"A sample of what?" asked Olivia.

"Of Sasquatch!" Noah laughed. "I believe this dart is designed to pierce an animal and then fall out, taking a piece of flesh and hair with it. It's a way of collecting a biopsy—a tiny cross-section of skin and meat—from a distance. But when it fell out, the doc couldn't find the sample. It would have given Skookum quite a sting, like the biggest bee he ever encountered. No wonder he wailed."

"But what would the doctor want with a piece of a Sasquatch?" Jayden demanded. He was angry that a person like a doctor would purposely hurt Skookum to collect a sample.

"Hmm... I'm not sure," answered Noah. "The sample could tell him many things, like the Bigfoot's blood type or cell structure or DNA. But it wouldn't help him prove the existence of the Sasquatch. He has nothing to compare it to. As far as I know, Skookum is the last of his kind..." Noah hesitated. "Unless..."

The campers waited several moments for Noah to finish his sentence. He was lost in thought. When he looked up at them, he seemed troubled. "If Skookum is the last Sasquatch, maybe Dr. Flintlock is trying to make a copy of him. He might be trying to collect a DNA sample so he can make a clone of Skookum!"

9. No Time for Dessert

Dozens of campers poured down the steps around Evan, Jayden, Olivia, Maddie and Noah. Lunch was over, and they had missed it. Several campers stopped to rub Murphie's ears and were rewarded with lots of slobbery drool. In minutes, everyone had gone off to their activities. Noah stood and said, "Let's see if we can find you some leftovers. And ask Nehemiah if he is free to talk with you about what happened this morning."

The four hungry campers gobbled down warmed-up soup and grilled cheese sandwiches. They paused only to answer Nehemiah's questions about where they had gone and why. He spoke in kind but serious tones. Nehemiah explained the trouble they had caused by disappearing without telling anyone.

"The biggest disappointment is that you intentionally disregarded Noah's instructions. He told you not to go into the woods without him." He glanced at Evan. "And I need to hold you responsible for this, Evan. Is it not true that these others were following your lead?"

Evan sighed. "Are you going to send me home?"

Nehemiah watched him and considered the question before answering. "I don't believe that sending you home will make you a better leader. What do you think would help?"

Evan looked down. "If I became a better follower?"

"I appreciate your answer, Evan," Nehemiah smiled. "One of the keys to good leadership is to learn to follow well. The times that I listened carefully and obeyed God were my best leadership moments. And worth the cost."

"So, what happens now?" asked Maddie.

Nehemiah thought for a moment and said, "You need to know that your actions have consequences. Evan was the one who led you wrong, but you all chose to follow him." He looked at his clipboard. "I want you to go to your activities this afternoon. Girls, you're at the challenge course; Evan and Jayden, at the climbing gym. However, I'll have you sit out the wide game this evening."

The campers gasped. The wide game? Not that! Jayden felt he could go all day without the climbing gym or challenge course. But the wide game...! They all looked at one another in dismay. After a moment, Evan said, "Okay. We understand. We trust your judgment."

Nehemiah seemed surprised. "Well, I must say that I am glad for your good attitude about this, Evan. We've watched you for several summers now, and we believe God has leadership in mind for you. It's good to see it grow."

They all thanked Nehemiah and went off to their activities, which had already started. The climbing gym was nothing like the one at Jayden's school, he realized as they put on their harnesses. It was made of real rock and had caves to explore as well as walls to climb. They even tried out a slackline high above the ground. It was way harder than it looked.

Jayden wondered why his friend was so okay with Nehemiah's decision. They would have to miss the wide game! He asked Evan about it as they walked from the climbing gym back to the cabin to put on their swim shorts. Evan shrugged. "Well, what else could I tell Nehemiah? He was right—I got you all in trouble. I'm just glad that nothing worse happened than missing the wide game tonight. I'm sorry you have to miss it too."

"But what about Skookum?" Jayden persisted.

"I don't know. We didn't actually help him, except by finding the dart. Noah will know what to do. I think we're done!"

Jayden wasn't satisfied with his friend's answer. Dr. Flintlock was still out searching for Skookum. If the doctor fired another shot at Skookum and collected a sample of his DNA, could he make a clone of the Bigfoot? And if he did, what would he do with it? Not set it free, that's for sure. It would be his experiment. A prisoner on display. Jayden couldn't let that happen.

Noah was in their cabin when they arrived. "I'm sad you won't be participating in the wide game," he told them. "I'll talk with Nehemiah. Perhaps we can find another way for you to be involved."

"Noah," said Jayden tentatively, "could Dr. Flintlock actually clone Skookum from a sample like the one we found?"

"Regrettably, yes," Noah frowned. "All he needs is one undamaged skin cell. He would remove its nucleus—where the DNA is stored—and transfer it into an egg that had its nucleus removed. The egg would have to be from a close relative; I'm not sure what would work. But yes, it could be done." As Noah walked out the door of the cabin, he called back, "Don't be too worried. Skookum will be all the more cautious now. The doctor has only a slim chance of finding him again."

The whole time the boys played on the waterfront slides and the Blob, Jayden worried about Skookum. He wondered if they would hear another rifle shot, which would tell them that the doctor had found him and collected a DNA sample. But they heard no gunshot that afternoon. As they returned to the cabin to get changed, Jayden realized he hadn't been as afraid of the water this time. Not even when a much bigger boy blobbed him into orbit before he landed in the cool water. Maybe his concern for Skookum made his usual fears fade in comparison.

They sat with Maddie and Olivia at dinner and moaned about the wide game they would miss. "I want to play so bad," complained Maddie. "This isn't the last game of the week, is it?"

"No," Evan assured her. "This is only our third day. We'll have at least one more." Third day? To Jayden, it felt like they had already been at camp for a week. So much happened every day. Three more nights after this one. Not much time to make sure Skookum was safe.

Nehemiah came and joined them at their table. "Now, I don't want you to think I have changed my mind about the consequences. However, I talked with Noah and we will have you help with the running of the game tonight."

The four campers' eyes lit up. "What will we do?" asked Olivia.

"I asked Esther to come and explain... And here she is!" Nehemiah stood and gave his chair to Esther, who had just arrived. She soon had the campers' full attention. Not only was she dazzlingly beautiful; she had a commanding, no-nonsense presence.

"Okay, so the job I am giving you is not easy!" she explained. "But I'm relying on you to get it right because tonight's game hangs on your attention to detail. Are you up for it?" The four campers gulped but nodded. "Aaaand..." she added, looking at her watch, "we don't have time to wait for dessert. Nuts, I love dessert. But we need to get out there and set up. Coming?"

That's how the four campers found themselves following Queenie Esther past the tantalizing scent of fresh apple pie and out the front doors. At first, they thought it was pretty cool to help the staff behind the scenes. But helping with the game turned out to be a lot of hard work. They set up props and posted signs. They sat at a table where they collected clues. And they gave out game coins to camper after camper until their heads were spinning.

When the bell rang to end the game and call everyone to chapel, the four campers collapsed on their tables. "That was exhausting!" said Maddie. "I'll never take a wide game for granted again." It took so long to clean up, the music had already started when they arrived at the big room upstairs. None of them had the energy to move a muscle to the music.

The speaker that evening was their cabin leader, Barney, who they had hardly seen all day. He winked at Jayden and Evan as the crowd of campers found cushions to sit on. Barney went right to the point. "What do you love?" he called out to the crowd. "Camp Liverwurst" came out strong and loud as the campers shouted back to him. Also mentioned were chocolate, my dog, Gaga ball and Noah's left big toe, among many other things.

"*Who* do you love?" was Barney's next question. Many campers bellowed out "mom" or "dad." Others shouted the names of celebrities, and a few names were called out that made their owners blush. Lots of people yelled "God" or "Jesus," and others called out the names of their cabin leaders.

When he had quieted the crowd, Barney had another question. "I heard some of you say you love God. Tell me, how do you do that?" No shouting this time. What a hard question! A few people offered answers that sounded okay to Jayden. Yet, he wondered if there was more to loving God than spending time with him or reading the Bible.

"I'm looking for a couple of volunteers, and you need to be best friends." Many hands went up. Barney chose two girls from the middle of the room whom Jayden didn't know. They went up to join Barney, arms linked and looking a bit nervous. Barney found out that their names were Lily and Isabella, and they lived in the same neighborhood. They liked basketball and watching funny videos on their phones.

"I'm glad you have one another as friends," said Barney. "Lily, I have a question for you. What if one day you were hanging out with your friend Isabella, and you found out that she is actually God? You know, the One who created the universe and dinosaurs and cute puppies. The Person who is currently keeping our planet in its orbit. And the One who gets to tell us what is good and what is bad."

Lily looked at Barney with big eyes and an open mouth that had nothing to say. Barney continued, "Would it make a difference to your friendship with Isabella if she was God?"

"Uh..." Lily laughed. "Yeah! Of course it would. I mean, I would still be her friend, but..."

"But, many things would be different," Barney finished for her. "For example, trusting that Isabella is *not* actually God, do you usually obey everything she commands you to do?"

Lily looked at Isabella. "Well, I like her and we do a lot of the same things together. But no, if she started bossing me around, I wouldn't like it. I wouldn't want to do everything she told me to. Sorry, Isabella!" Her friend smiled and shrugged.

"Okay, let me read something that Jesus once said and our friend John wrote down. Jesus was telling his students that the greatest love a person can have for one's friend is to die for them. Does that sound about right?" The girls nodded. "But then he said to them, 'You are my friends if you do what I command.' What do you think of that?"

After a moment, Isabella said, "I think it's different

than me bossing Lily around. It's okay for Jesus to tell us what to do. He's God and we should obey him."

"I agree," said Barney. "So, being a friend of God won't be the same as being a friend to Lily, will it? We should love people, and we should love God. But loving God will look different from loving people." He gave the girls high-fives. "Thanks for your help, Lily and Isabella."

As the girls went back to their cushions, Barney said, "Does anyone have a new answer to the question I asked earlier? How does a person love God?" Lots of hands went up.

The campers had many good answers. One said we love God by trusting him, and another that we love God by obeying him. A cabin leader said that we love God when we love the people he made. Emma said if we love Jesus, we will do the same kinds of things he did. When Nabil stood up to give an answer, everyone listened carefully. "Anybody can love their friends," he said. "But those who love God will love even their enemies." Jayden knew Nabil's story and was sure he was speaking from experience.

"Wow," said Barney, "your answers to my question are on a whole new level now! Maybe you learned something this evening. Don't expect friendship with God to look exactly like a friendship with people! He will want you to trust him completely and do what he tells you. Not because you have to, but because you want to. Because you love him."

Barney kept talking for a few minutes more about what a great friend Jesus is. Jayden was thinking hard about the enemy thing. Love an enemy? How could he love someone like Dr. Flintlock? He was angry that the doctor was trying to track down Skookum for his own selfish reasons. He didn't deserve love.

As they were walking back to their cabin, Jayden asked Evan what he thought about Barney's talk. "I can't imagine that God would want us to love a person like Dr. Flintlock!" Jayden complained. "Shouldn't we try to stop him?"

"Maybe stopping the doctor would be a way to love him," answered Evan.

Jayden hadn't thought of that. He was about to reply when they both stopped dead in their tracks. A long, eerie, despairing wail came from the direction of the mountain. They heard a gunshot, and then silence.

10. The Unexpected Answer

Jayden and Evan stared at one another for a moment, then raced toward the cabin. Before they arrived, Noah met them on the path. "Evan! Jayden! Thank God you're safe!"

"You heard, right?" panted Jayden. "Skookum... and a rifle shot..." He was sure Noah would want them to do nothing about it. But he was wrong.

"We're taking a night hike," answered Noah. "Put on some sturdy shoes and meet me on the front steps of the Lodge."

Evan cheered. "You mean it's time, Noah?"

"Yep, it's time! We need to find the doctor, as soon as we can. Go join the others and be ready in five minutes." He walked quickly in the direction they had just come from.

"Noah!" Jayden called after him. "What'll we do with the doctor when we find him?"

Noah turned and answered, "That's something I want you to think about, Jayden. What would be the best thing to do with our friend the doctor?" He strode away.

"Friend?" Jayden said to Evan as they hurried to the cabin. "Enemy is more like it. I don't have a clue what to do with him. Put him in jail? Take away his gun?"

"That's why Noah told you to think about it, Jayden!" said Evan. "Maybe the first thing that comes to mind isn't the best thing." Just then, they reached the cabin. Their cabinmates were scurrying to find their shoes and pull on hoodies.

"There you are," said Barney as they entered. "Did you see Noah on your way here? Good. Leaving in two minutes." He handed them headlamps and whistles. Evan had hiking boots, but Jayden had only his sneakers. He hoped they would do. When the group reached the Lodge, Abigail and Mary's cabin group were there too.

Noah called the two cabin groups and their leaders together. "Everyone ready? Good shoes? Something warm to wear? An excellent night for an adventure!"

"Are we really trying to find the Bigfoot?" asked one of the girls in a trembling voice.

"Good question, Zoe. No, we're not!" answered Noah. "Skookum has had enough trauma this week. But we have an intruder on our mountain, a researcher named Dr. Flintlock, who's making life difficult for our Sasquatch friend. Our mission tonight is to find the doctor and convince him to leave Skookum alone. I'm counting on you because I believe we can do those two things better together."

Evan spoke up. "Why do you think we'll find him tonight when we haven't been able to during the day?"

Noah adjusted his headlamp. "We attached a small camera to Zesi, John's eagle friend, and with it we spotted a campfire at a point about halfway up the mountain. We're sure this is where we'll find the doctor.

We'll quietly surround him, and when we arrive at his campfire, he will have nowhere to go."

"Will it be safe, Noah?" asked Emma. "I'm kinda scared."

Noah smiled. "Safe? Nothing worth doing is perfectly safe in this world, Emma. But we'll do our best to keep the risks small. We travel together tonight, always within sight of each other's headlamp. If you're hurt, or lost or even scared, blow on your whistle and everyone will come to where you are."

Everyone soon removed their hoodies as they trekked up the mountain. Jayden couldn't see how they would sneak up on Dr. Flintlock this way. The group was noisy and lit up like a string of Christmas lights. But they did look awesome. Jayden wouldn't want to walk through these woods at night by himself. But he felt okay in the middle of the crowd of campers.

His sneakers were giving him trouble, though. The way became rough. Tree roots twisted across the path. He found the steep, rocky bits hard to navigate with no grip on his shoes. Jayden struggled to keep up with Evan, who was now well ahead of him. But the person behind him was even slower, so Jayden was by himself as he climbed up the mountain. He didn't like it. He was deciding whether he should try and catch up with Evan, or wait for the person behind him, when it happened.

So many things took place at the same time. His ankle rolled under him on a tree root. Gasping in pain, he felt his other foot slip off the path. As he fell, his head hit a branch and his headlamp went flying. And then he was tumbling downhill through the bushes in the dark until he smacked against the trunk of a tree. The blow knocked the wind out of him and he sprawled on the ground in the blackness. The people who were behind him didn't see anything. They passed by as he gasped to regain his breath. Everything went completely quiet.

As soon as he was able to sit up, Jayden reached for the whistle on a string around his neck. But the string came loose in his hands and there was no whistle. He tried to yell, but not much came out because he was still winded. When he tried to stand to his feet, he would have screamed if he could, his ankle hurt so bad. Finally, he leaned back against the tree and thought about each breath, one at a time. Soon, he was able to breathe normally again.

It was utterly dark. Jayden waved his hand in front of his face and could see nothing. He looked up and faintly saw the outline of the treetops against the almost-black sky. A single star twinkled at him. It could not guide him even if he knew how to read the stars. At least the night was warm. He pulled his hoody back on anyway. He had no idea what else to do.

Jayden cried for a while. His ankle stung if he moved it even a tiny bit. He was alone on a mountainside in the dark and not one person knew where he was. Had the group even noticed he was missing yet? He thought back over the day. How could it be the same century when he and his cabin group learned how to wakesurf, let alone the same day? The longest day ever.

As he sat in the dark, he became more aware of all

the small noises around him. The more noises he heard, the bigger was the creature he imagined making them. But nothing happened. After an anxious while, he realized that all the flutterings, creakings and rustlings around him were nothing to worry about. In fact, the longer he waited in the dark, the less he was afraid. He could do nothing about his situation. He could only wait and see what happened.

As he thought about this, something came to mind that he could do. But he wasn't sure if he wanted to. For the last three days, he had lived with a group of people who believed in God and followed Jesus. It was a whole new experience for him. What he noticed the most was that they talked with God like he was really there. Could he talk with God too? Would it make any difference if he asked for God's help?

Well, why not? The worst that could happen was nothing at all, which was what he already had. If God ever wanted an opportunity to prove himself, here it was. Jayden knew about closing his eyes to pray, but he wasn't sure what to do with his hands. In the end, he held his arms up in the air like he had seen Peter do on the first day. It took a long time to decide how to start, but eventually he spoke words aloud to the Someone he couldn't see.

"Hey God, if you're there you can tell I'm in trouble. Nobody knows I'm hurt or where I am. Would you please send somebody—anybody—to find me and help me? If it's not too much trouble, could it be soon? Thanks a lot. Ummm... take care. This is Jayden, by the way." People say a special word at the end of their prayers, but Jayden couldn't remember what it was. Oh well. He waited to see if anything would happen.

It would be wrong to say that nothing happened. Jayden did feel a bit better after speaking out about the mess he was in and asking for help. He felt more and more like everything would turn out okay. But nothing else happened for a long time. He could no longer see the one star through the trees and he felt the prickle of tears forming in his eyes again.

It was then that he heard a noise. It was unlike the night sounds all around him. This came from a specific direction. It was like something was trying to be quiet but was too big not to be noticed. He remembered Noah's warning about the animals that—when he wasn't around—would act like any wild animal. He wished Noah was with him. No doubt, a very large something was moving cautiously toward him.

The whatever-it-was stopped only a few feet away. He could hear it breathing—great, deep breaths—and there was a smell like his uncle's sheep barn. Jayden couldn't move. He couldn't yell. He could hardly even breathe. The creature moved toward him again, then sat down with a sigh and leaned back against Jayden's tree. It was so massive, he felt the tree move slightly.

When the creature reached out and touched his hand, Jayden almost fainted. It took Jayden's hand in its own. Its hand was so unbelievably huge, his own hand was like a tiny baby's in comparison. The creature gently squeezed Jayden's hand, three times. This immediately brought tears to Jayden's eyes because his mom used to do that. Sit down beside him and squeeze his hand. Three times.

Jayden had no doubt about what was sitting beside him in the dark. "Skookum, is that really you?" Another squeeze of his hand. He knew he should be absolutely terrified. Sitting beside him and holding his hand was a gigantic beast that most people thought was a myth or the subject of a horror film. But he wasn't afraid. He had asked God to send someone—anyone— to find him, and God chose Skookum. He knew everything would be okay. Jayden wasn't sure if that said more about Skookum or more about God.

"Skookum, I don't know if you can understand me..." Jayden felt the Bigfoot shift slightly as if it was trying to listen. Like a dog does when it tilts its head. "I'm hurt and I can't move, and I need to go find my group. Skookum, I need Noah!"

Skookum squeezed his hand again. Jayden wondered that a creature so big and strong could be so gentle. His amazement was even greater when he heard Skookum say, "NO-AH."

Jayden's heart skipped a beat. He squeezed the Bigfoot's hand. "Yes, Skookum! Noah. Can you take me to him? Skookum, take me to Noah!"

Skookum let go of Jayden's hand. The creature moaned and shook his huge head. But a few moments later, Jayden heard him get up in the dark. He felt Skookum's breath as he reached down and took Jayden's hand again and began to pull him to his feet. Jayden gave a yell; his ankle hurt so bad, he couldn't help it. Skookum let go in surprise and Jayden lowered himself back to the tree. "I'm sorry, Skookum! I'm hurt. I can't walk with you."

In the dark, Skookum knelt down in front of Jayden. He heard him sniffing around his legs. His huge hands carefully encased Jayden's hurt foot. His hands were cool and soft and felt wonderful, wrapped around Jayden's throbbing ankle. "Wow, Skookum! Thanks. Yes, that's where it hurts. Though how you knew that, I have no idea." The longer the Sasquatch held his foot, the better it felt until the throbbing died away.

Jayden couldn't help a moment of panic when he suddenly felt Skookum's arm reach under him and pick him up. The Bigfoot held him against his hairy chest like a small child. Jayden sensed rather than saw that he was high above the ground. One of Skookum's hands was still wrapped around his ankle to hold it steady. They began to move through the woods at an astounding pace.

Jayden would never forget the race up the mountainside in the dark, carried by Skookum the Bigfoot. They dodged around trees, leaped over streams and bounded up rockfaces. When the forest opened, Jayden could see by starlight the outline of Skookum's shaggy head above him. It was all so impossible, Jayden began to laugh.

The sound startled Skookum, who stopped and glanced at him with concern. "It's okay, Skookum!" The Bigfoot started running again. "I'm just... so happy... that you... you were... sent to... find me... and it's all... just... so... crazy!" Well, that's how it sounded as Jayden jostled up and down in Skookum's arms. The sound of his own voice made Jayden laugh all the more.

In a few minutes, Skookum slowed down. Jayden became aware of the glow of a campfire through the trees up ahead. The Bigfoot moved cautiously forward, always in the shadows, until they were nearly at the small clearing. The fire lit up the trees all around. Skookum gently set Jayden down where he could see, but not be seen. He took Jayden's hand and placed in it something that felt familiar.

Before him was a strange sight. In the center of the clearing sat Dr. Flintlock on a tiny folding chair. On the other side of the fire, Noah sat on the ground, speaking in a low voice. All around the clearing stood Barney, Abigail, Mary and their campers. No one noticed Jayden and Skookum standing in the shadows behind them. Well, Jayden anyway. Leaning against a tree, Jayden looked back and saw that Skookum had quietly vanished into the night.

11. Believing is Seeing

Jayden stayed where he was. He strained to hear the conversation by the campfire between Noah and the doctor. It didn't seem to be going well.

The doctor was angry. "What makes you think that surrounding me in my private camping spot will deter me?" he was saying. He looked around at the campers. "A group of school children! Is this your plan for intimidating me?" he laughed.

"It's not our purpose to intimidate you," answered Noah in a voice gentler than the doctor's. "We came to get your attention. And to reason with you."

"If that was your purpose, you should have sent someone with the required intellectual capacity." His words drew a murmur of anger from the campers in the circle. "I will not bandy words with some ancient zookeeper."

Noah held up his hand to quiet the campers' indignation. "I see," he said, "You think your scientific data and achievements make you smarter than me."

"In a nutshell, yes!" the doctor replied. "How can you be expected to understand the enormous importance of analyzing this amazing creature! Just think of it—a Sasquatch, living here on this mountain. Researching this beast could result in the most amazing discoveries. We might discover a distant relative of ours, a missing link! We could fill in vast gaps in evolutionary theory."

"If it was only knowledge you wanted, I would help you," replied Noah calmly. "But I believe you want more. Why should you study a tiny sample from a Sasquatch when you could replicate your own? Am I right that you will attempt to make a clone of Skookum? And failing that, collect him as a specimen?"

"Don't give the creature a name, as if it is an intelligent being!" the doctor exploded. "Yes, of course! Why would I not seek to preserve this animal when we may never find another like it? I admit it—I will obtain a sufficient sample and attempt to clone the Bigfoot. Or capture the creature itself. It will be my greatest achievement!"

Jayden became more and more enraged the longer he listened. Finally, he had enough. Taking a stick from the ground to support himself, he hopped out into the open and confronted the doctor. The sight of this scratched, rumpled, stinky and furious boy made Dr. Flintlock shrink back in his tiny chair.

"Skookum *is* intelligent!" Jayden shouted. "Maybe more intelligent than you, and you call yourself a doctor!" His fury made him lose his balance. As he swayed on one leg, his friend Evan ran to his side to steady him. Olivia and Maddie joined them. But Jayden never took his blazing eyes off the doctor, who looked alarmed.

"Jayden, praise God you are safe!" exclaimed Noah, getting to his feet. "And he's not only safe—he's on fire!

Did Skookum find you?"

Jayden nodded. "Which is why I know that Skookum is not some dumb animal, Dr. Flintlock! Even if he was, that wouldn't give you the right to hurt him or use him for research." Jayden told the story of how he became separated from the group. How he was injured and lost on the dark mountainside. "Skookum came and found me, Doctor! If you were eight feet tall and wanted to help a little kid who was lost in the woods, what would you do? Would you know how to approach him without scaring him to death?"

He told the doctor about how Skookum sat down and shared his tree. How he took Jayden's hand until he wasn't so freaked out. "By the time he picked me up to carry me here, I wasn't afraid at all anymore. I trusted him, far more than I trust you, Dr. Flintlock!"

Up until then, the doctor had listened to him, intrigued by his story. Here he interrupted, "Wait a minute! Are you telling me that creature carried you here just now? Where is he?"

Dr. Flintlock reached for his gun case, but Noah moved it out of reach with his foot. "Not so fast, doctor! I am sure Skookum is long gone by now. And you need to listen to this boy's story. I believe he has more to teach you."

"Indeed?" sneered the doctor. "I think he is a little liar! Another foolish attempt to get rid of me. Tell me, boy—how did the Sasquatch know to bring you here from wherever you were lost on the mountain?"

Jayden hesitated, unsure if he should tell this part of the story. He looked at Noah, who nodded. "I talked with him, Doctor. I told Skookum I was hurt and lost. And I asked him to bring me to Noah."

The doctor snorted. "So you let him pick you up and carry you? How on earth could you know that this brute animal understood you? He might have taken you anywhere!"

"I knew because..." replied Jayden. "Because... he said Noah's name."

There was complete silence for a moment as Jayden's words sunk in, and then a sudden buzz of excited voices all around the circle. Skookum could talk? The doctor waved his arms for silence, but it took some time before the campers calmed down.

"You tell me, boy, that this creature spoke to you?" he asked.

"Well, only one word, but yes. I asked him to take me to Noah. A moment later, I clearly heard him say, 'No-ah.' He seemed upset at first, like he understood me but didn't want to go. He moaned and shook himself. But then he stood and tried to help me to my feet." Jayden explained how Skookum sniffed to figure out that he was hurt, and how he held Jayden's ankle securely. "And speaking of ankles, can I sit down now? Mine really aches." His friends helped him to the ground and sat with him.

Dr. Flintlock stood and paced across the circle. He was talking to himself. "It can speak? Not necessarily a sign of intelligence, but is it possible? That would be the most extraordinary..." Then he broke off and said angrily, "Bah! I don't believe it! Not a word of it." He turned and pointed at Jayden. "You...! You never saw any Bigfoot, and it certainly didn't carry you here! What evidence do you have? Why should I believe you?"

In response, Jayden began taking off his sneaker. Evan, Olivia and Maddie helped him loosen the lacing. They gently removed the shoe while supporting his ankle. It hurt a lot, but it had to happen. The sock was even more difficult, but they managed to carefully peel it off. Underneath, his ankle was a brilliant shade of purple and quite swollen.

As his friends helped him, Jayden said, "You're right, Doctor. I never saw the Bigfoot. It was too dark to see anything, except the shape of his head in the starlight. But I did hear him speak. I felt him squeeze my hand, and I definitely smelled him."

"You still smell like him, I think," said Olivia. Everyone laughed.

Jayden continued. "If that's not enough evidence for you, doctor, how did I make it here through the woods on an ankle that looks like this?" The doctor didn't say anything. Instead, he took a small towel and poured his water bottle out on it. Then he wrung it out and wrapped it around Jayden's ankle.

When he was done, Jayden said, "Thank you. And if that's still not enough, I have a present for you from Skookum." He held out a blue cylinder with an orange cap.

The doctor took the cylinder and examined it. The needle was not covered in hair or blood like the last one, but was bent and broken at the tip. "Where did you get this?" he said in wonder. "I knew it didn't hit him. I heard it strike a tree. But that must have been a mile or more from here!"

"I told you," explained Jayden. "Skookum handed it to me, right behind that big tree. I guess he wanted you to have it back. Maybe he's saying, No thanks! I'm not interested!"

The doctor chuckled and shook his head. "Unbelievable. But I can think of no other explanation. You must have been with the Bigfoot. Not only did he not hurt you; he helped you and seems to have communicated with you. This is most astonishing."

"So, does that mean you'll leave Skookum alone now?" demanded Jayden.

"Is that what you expect of me?" asked the doctor, frowning.

Jayden thought for a moment and said, "No, I don't think it's enough to just leave him alone. Shouldn't you be trying to protect him? All you've done so far is shoot at him, twice! What good is that to Skookum? You should be, I don't know, like a gamekeeper for him. Keep people from bothering him."

Dr. Flintlock looked impressed with Jayden's idea. "That's true! I could become the first-ever Sasquatch conservationist! Since most people think it is a fictitious beast, current research is minimal and there are no protections for this creature. I could ensure the preservation of his habitat! Study the effects of human interaction and climate change on this species..."

Noah interrupted. "All well and good, doctor. But don't forget, Skookum lives on our mountain. And you are a trespasser on our—and his—property. Even with the best of intentions, aren't you still trying to make a name for yourself? Without concern for the effect on those around you?"

"Ah, here it is!" sneered the doctor, changing his tone. "The zookeeper objects to scientific study! I know your kind—you blindly believe in a God you can't see, while closing your eyes to the *facts*. Your belief is illogical and without any empirical proof! Give me clear, testable evidence of your God, and then I will know if I should believe in him!"

All the campers were closely watching this exchange between Noah and Dr. Flintlock. Jayden had called the doctor less intelligent than Skookum. Now he thought the doctor sounded smart. How would Noah answer the doctor's challenge? How can you know for sure that God exists?

Noah smiled. "As a zookeeper, I am surprised at the shift in our conversation! We went from protecting Sasquatches to proving God. Well done, doctor! Though I am not sure why you accept the existence of a fictitious creature, but not the existence of God."

"Evidence, my good man! It's all about the evidence!"

"I agree, but you have it the wrong way around. You're ready to believe in God once all the evidence proves his existence. I can guarantee you'll never get there. A friend of mine once said, 'By faith we understand that the world was created by the word of God, so that what is seen was not made out of things that can be seen.'"

"I don't get your point, man!" the doctor said

impatiently.

"I'm glad to explain, but I don't expect you to understand," said Noah sadly. "You think that seeing is believing. But it's the other way around: believing is seeing." Noah sighed. "You're an intelligent man with much knowledge. But you will never see things as they truly are until you have faith in the One who made them, and who made you."

The doctor didn't reply, and it was silent around the clearing. Jayden liked Noah's answer: believing is seeing. He would have to think more about that.

"Well, everyone," said Noah, "it's very late—it's tomorrow, actually, if I'm not mistaken! Time we headed back to camp. Doctor, you are welcome to come back with us and we'll find you a comfortable bed to sleep in tonight. But tomorrow we must ask you to leave this property and not return uninvited. Are we clear about that?"

The doctor looked anything but comfortable with the idea. "If it's all the same to you, I would prefer to stay here tonight," he muttered. Straightening himself, he said, "But I will come to your Lodge tomorrow to take my leave of you, for now."

"Fair enough," replied Noah. Turning to Jayden, he said, "So, how do we get you down this mountain? I don't suppose Skookum is still around..." He was interrupted by a joyous bark. Not Skookum, but Murphie the Newfoundland dog bounded into the clearing and nearly knocked Noah over.

Behind him came several of the camp staff. They looked surprised at the sight of the campfire and the people standing around it. "Well met!" panted Nehemiah. "We were starting to wonder if everything was okay with you, so we chased after Murphie all the way up here."

He stared at the doctor. Noah said, "Nehemiah, meet Dr. Robert Flintlock, who has been studying our friend Skookum. Doctor Flintlock, Nehemiah, our camp director." They nodded to one another. "Well then, I'm sure we can take turns carrying Jayden down the hill. But let's first stabilize your ankle. Dr. Luke, would you..."

"Hey Jayden, good to see you again!" smiled Dr. Luke, who went down on his knees to unwrap the towel and examine his ankle. "Another memorable wipeout, I presume? I bet this one has a great story to go with it!" So Jayden got to tell his adventure with Skookum again while Dr. Luke bound up his ankle with a splint and cold packs. Every time he told the story, the more Jayden saw things about it that were so impossible. Unless... unless it was God who sent Skookum to him. Like Noah had said, if only he could believe in God, this whole night would make a lot more sense.

As soon as they arrived back at the cabin and had a bit of a snack, everyone dropped right off to sleep. What a long day it had been! And three more days to go before the end of camp. Jayden lay awake for a while, partly because of the pain in his ankle, but mostly because his heart was so full. It was enough that he had been rescued by a real, live Sasquatch! But what he couldn't get over was how he had confronted Dr.

Flintlock in front of all his friends.

And wondering how on earth so much could have changed in three days, he slept. Jayden didn't wake again until the sun was streaming full on his face.

12. A Never-Ending Journey

"How does your ankle feel this morning?"

Jayden struggled to open his eyes so he could see who was talking. The day was so bright, it took him a moment to focus on Barney's face. "Um, it's okay..." He stopped short, gasping with the sudden sharp pain. "...unless I move it."

"I bet," Barney said sympathetically. "What a night we had! I'm sure you're hungry—it's nearly eleven. When Martha the Cook heard what happened, she went all out."

Jayden half sat up and looked around. The cabin was empty except for Barney and Evan. His friend was holding a big tray with cinnamon rolls, bacon and eggs, fried potatoes and orange juice. It was way too much for Jayden, so he shared it with Evan and Barney. They insisted that he take all the bacon.

"Where are the rest of the guys?" Jayden asked between mouthfuls.

"The girls' cabin wanted a rematch of archery tag," replied Evan. "They said it would be more 'even' without your arrow-grabbing skills. But the guys are getting thrashed." Jayden laughed but felt a pang of regret. His hurt ankle meant no more running around this week.

"Dr. Luke will be by shortly to look at your ankle," Barney told him. "He thinks it's not broken, only a bad sprain, which I am sorry to say can be even more painful." He set the tray on the table. "Don't worry—we'll do our best to make the rest of your week awesome!"

When Dr. Luke arrived, Barney and Evan left to rescue the guys in archery tag. The doctor unwrapped Jayden's ankle and was happy to see it was less swollen, though now green and blue in addition to purple. After gentle pushing and prodding, he said. "No, I believe it's not broken, but you should still have an x-ray done when you get home." The ankle felt better when he bound it up again, and the ice packs were like heaven.

"Dr. Luke," began Jayden hesitantly, "I've been thinking about the stuff you told me—you know, the last time I was hurt. About not needing to be afraid anymore."

"Right," Dr. Luke replied. "I got carried away with my favorite story—when Jesus overcame death. So, tell me what you've been thinking."

"Well, when I was up on the mountain alone in the dark, I should have been freaked out of my mind. But I wasn't, somehow. I knew I would be okay because I asked God to send me someone. I didn't expect him to send me a Sasquatch!" Jayden laughed. "But even then, I wasn't scared. It's so weird."

"I don't think it's weird," Dr. Luke replied. "I think you're on a journey, and the destination at the end of this road is faith in God." He put another pillow under Jayden's leg to raise his ankle a little higher. "I should tell you that the way ahead of you is not an easy one, but a good one. In fact, it's the best."

"My dad told me not to come home with a bunch of weird ideas about God." Jayden frowned. "I'm worried about what he'll think of me when I tell him what happened here. What do you think I should say?"

"You should tell him the truth," Dr. Luke smiled. "But remember, your dad is on the same journey. He just hasn't come nearly as far and won't understand as much as you."

"My dad? Serious?" Jayden was surprised. "I don't think so—he's against everything religious. Sometimes I think he's against the whole world."

"That tells me he's walking this road while kicking and screaming, but walking it nonetheless," said Dr. Luke, as he stood up. "I think it's time to get you out of this cabin. Are you ready?" Dr. Luke showed him how to use a pair of crutches to move around the room, then took him outside. Jayden laughed. Parked at the steps was a small ATV. "It's only for getting around, okay?" said Dr. Luke. "The governor is set to low, so you won't go fast. I hope you have fun, though!"

What a riot Jayden had that day! True, he didn't get to do many of the activities, but the ATV was a big hit everywhere he went. He gave so many people rides (at the speed of a fast walk) that he had to ask Solomon three times for more gas. And so many people asked him about his night adventure with Skookum the Sasquatch, his voice gave out by mid-afternoon.

Dr. Luke found Jayden and asked him how his ankle felt. He had no voice to answer, so the doctor made him go lie down in the cabin until dinnertime. His friend Evan gave up his chance to try the new big rope swing at the lake to be with him.

"Sorry you were hurt, Jayden," he said. "It's not the week you thought it would be."

"Are you joking?" Jayden's voice went sky-high. "My week has been perfect! The best one of my life."

"Man, was I scared when we arrived at Dr. Flintlock's campfire and I couldn't find you," Evan recalled. "I didn't have Noah's faith that you were okay. Do you think he figured Skookum would track you down?"

"Maybe. Anyway, I *was* okay, mostly, and Skookum did find me," Jayden croaked. "I wonder where he is now?"

"I asked Noah about that at breakfast," said Evan. "He thinks Skookum has returned to his cave on the mountain and we won't see any sign of him again this week."

"And Dr. Flintlock...?"

"He hasn't shown up here yet today," Evan replied. "I wonder if he will. And if Skookum is safe from him."

They talked and played Settlers for the rest of the afternoon until they heard the bell for dinner. When they pulled up in front of the Lodge on the ATV, Noah was on the stairs talking with Dr. Flintlock. The doctor was wearing his camouflage gear and backpack. He looked out of place in the middle of the stream of shorts-and-T-shirt campers clambering up the steps.

"Ah, there you are," said Noah. Jayden navigated the

stairs with his crutches, Evan spotting him so he didn't go over backward. "Dr. Flintlock was asking for you. He's joining us for dinner—let's sit at a table together." They found a small table near the window.

"How is the ankle today?" Dr. Flintlock began. "Still quite sore, I imagine."

"Well, I still can't put any weight on it," Jayden answered. "But I've had such a fun day, it hasn't bothered me so much."

"Yes, I saw you on the ATV." He paused, wringing his hands, and continued, "Jayden, I've had time today to think about your words. You have given me much to consider."

"What have you decided to do about Skookum?" Jayden asked.

"Stay silent, for a start," the doctor replied. "I can truthfully say that I searched for the Sasquatch and did not find him. Because, like you, I never had a good look at him. And because of you, I have no samples to take back with me." As they ate, the doctor outlined some other plans. He wanted to study the Sasquatch's habits and food supply. He would also seek legal protection for his habitat, and perhaps for the creature itself.

"That's awesome, doctor!" Jayden exclaimed. "Can you do all that?"

"We will see what the zookeeper permits," he replied, looking at Noah.

Noah laughed. "Just don't get carried away, doctor. I believe your fascination with Skookum may have turned a corner. But we will be keeping an eye on you, never fear."

The rest of Jayden's week at camp flew by so fast it was like it happened all in one day. The guys in his cabin helped him to the top of the big zipline and he soared over the treetops down the mountainside. A burly cabin leader named Andrew took Jayden and his friends sailing. When the wind died, they cast their lines in and caught three big trout. Jayden helped the staff with running the wide games. Olivia's cabin won in the end, just like she predicted. He even joined the final round of archery tag, though it was too hard to catch arrows while riding the ATV.

At the end of one long day, he gave Barney a lift back to the cabin. Murphie the Newfie, who had taken to following him everywhere, loped along beside them. When he turned off the ATV, Jayden spoke. "Barney, I just realized that I went this whole day without being afraid or worried about anything." He pulled out his crutches but remained seated. "I love it here! I can't believe it will all be over soon."

"Over?" Barney laughed and climbed off the ATV. "No, it's never over. Everything changes, but it never ends."

Jayden looked at him thoughtfully as he rubbed Murphie's ears. "Barney, can I ask you a question?" He hesitated. "If you're from Bible times, you must have died once."

Barney smiled. "Yes. Long ago, I experienced death. Most people have, you know."

"What was it like?" asked Jayden.

Barney laughed as he reached over and rumpled

Jayden's hair. "No spoilers! If I could tell you even half of what it was like to die, you couldn't grasp it." He smiled wistfully. "All I will tell you is that on the other side there was Someone who had been waiting all my life to welcome me *home*."

Whenever Jayden later thought about their conversation, the word "home" gave him a strange sense of hope and longing. Not "home" like where he and his dad lived, or Evan's house or camp or even what it was like when his mom was still around. Home, the way Barney said it, was a place so much better, the place where he belonged. Where Jesus was.

But in the meantime, the days and hours of his first week at Camp Liverwurst slipped away like the swirl of a canoe paddle. And then it was time to leave. At breakfast on the last morning, Peter stood and called out, "Who had the best time this week?" Along with shouts of "Me!" and "Everyone," Jayden heard a few people shout his name. Maddie yelled "Skookum!" at the top of her voice.

Peter continued, "Well, I've been coming here every summer for practically forever, and I think this week was one of the best yet!" Lots of screams and yells of agreement. When it died down, he said, "But one thing I know for sure: the best is yet to come!" The room erupted again.

"I know, I know, it is hard to leave a place as incredible as camp and we will shed a few tears today." Peter smiled around at the now-quiet campers. "Some of you wish you could stay here always. But that would be missing the point of camp. We brought you to this special place for one week so you could learn to walk with God back at home for the rest of your lives. What counts is what you do with what you have gained here."

And then they returned to the cabin to clean up and pack their stuff. Before he knew it, Jayden was driving the little ATV down the ramp to the dock where Noah's boat was moored. Animals of every description rambled and flew and slithered by him and up the gangplank. The water was perfectly still and emerald green, reflecting the mountains across the lake. But it's not over, Jayden reminded himself sternly.

He watched Evan having a conversation with Noah on the deck of the boat. Evan seemed a bit upset about something, but nodded his head as Noah left him to start the engine. When Barney had helped him up the gangplank, Jayden asked Evan, "What was that about?"

Evan looked up at him and gave a half-smile. "Noah thinks my time at Camp Liverwurst is nearing its end."

"Well, duh!" said Jayden. "We're all leaving today!"

"No, I mean... next summer will be my last summer here, for good."

"What? Why?" Jayden demanded.

"Because I will be old enough to be a leader soon, and... well, all the leaders at Camp Liverwurst are from the Bible, which I'm not," replied Evan. "Noah wants me to volunteer as a junior leader next summer at a small camp close to where we live. I can still come here as well next year, but that will be my last week at Camp Liverwurst."

Jayden didn't know what to say at first, and they

stared at the water swirling from the big propeller. Finally he said, "We just need to remember what Peter told us this morning, Evan. The whole point of Camp Liverwurst is to make us more ready for life in the real world." Jayden sighed. "I sure will miss this place, though."

Evan nodded. "So, are you coming back here with me next summer?"

"Wouldn't miss it for the..." But Jayden didn't get to finish his sentence. Murphie knocked them both over in pursuit of a monkey that had swiped his chew toy. Evan joined the chase all over the deck while Jayden watched and laughed. The boat slipped away from the dock, leaving Camp Liverwurst behind in the morning mist.

Also in this series by Jim Badke:

Camp Liverwurst & the Stray Compass

Maddie isn't sure who she is anymore.

Camp Liverwurst is still
Maddie's favorite place
ever. But everything seems
different this year,
including Maddie. Now
her new cabin leader wants
to take them on an epic
adventure. No friends,

snow in summer, a wobbly boat and baffling
creatures—what could possibly go wrong?

Camp Liverwurst and the Stray Compass is Book 2 in the
new *Camp Liverwurst* series of short read-aloud novels
for middle-school kids about camp.

Cabin leaders, teachers and parents will find that each
chapter can spark a dialogue about Jesus.

Included are questions and activities to prompt Bible
discussions about faith in God and self-identity.

-- Available from Amazon --

ISBN 978-1-7777101-2-5

Discussion Questions

If you are a camper, this section will help you think about each chapter. The goal is to decide what you will do about what you are learning.

If you are a cabin leader, you can use these questions and activities as a guide (not a script!) for discussion to help campers process the chapters you read to them. Plan on reading two to three chapters per day—for cabin devotions, during wake-up, after a meal or on a break.

Each set of questions has three parts:
1. **Ready** – Questions or an activity to help campers get ready to discuss God's word with you.
2. **Set** – Questions to set in their minds the big idea of a Bible passage (see the headings for each chapter below).
3. **Go** – Questions or an activity to help them decide what to do about what they learned.

Chapter 1 – God wraps himself around us and our fears.
1. **Ready** – Tell us how you first started coming to this camp. What are you most looking forward to this week? What kinda freaks you out?
2. **Set** – Psalm 139:1-6 (or more). How do you feel about the idea that God is all around you?
3. **Go** – Either on rocks or pieces of paper, each person writes down a personal worry or a fear. Have them pull a pair of clean socks from their bag and wrap up the worry/fear in it to remind them of the surrounding presence of God.

Chapter 2 – It is more helpful to build than destroy.

1. **Ready** – Who (and what) lives at your house? Tell us about your best day ever.
2. **Set** – Ephesians 4:29. What is easier: wrecking something or building something? How do you feel when someone uses words to build you up and encourage you?
3. **Go** – Talk about each person in the group, one at a time. Say something you like about that person or ask them a friendly question.

Chapter 3 – Love is the best target in life.

1. **Ready** – What is your target in life? What is the mark you often miss?
2. **Set** – Mark 12:28-31. What kind of "love" is Jesus talking about? Do you think it is easy or hard to hit the target called love? Why?
3. **Go** – Make a plan to do a random act of kindness for someone at camp tomorrow.

Chapter 4 – A person can love and fear God at the same time.

1. **Ready** – What would you attempt to do if you knew you were invincible like a superhero? Why would you not try it without superpowers?
2. **Set** – Proverbs 9:10. Think of an example of how a person who fears God might act differently than a person who is afraid of God. Do you think a person who fears God can also love him? How?
3. **Go** – Tell us about someone you know who loves and fears God. Do you want to be like them?

Chapter 5 – The natural world tells us about God.

1. **Ready** – Give each camper a nature object—a stone, branch, grass, picture of the sun, glass of water, etc. Each person explains to the group what it tells them about God. You may have to start them with an example.

2. **Set** – Psalm 19:1-3. How does the sky speak without making a sound? What does the night sky say about God?

3. **Go** – How much do you need God? Imagine standing between two towns. One is called "I-Don't-Need-God-At-All" and the other "I-Need-God-A-Lot." Which one are you closer to? How close?

Chapter 6 – The story of Jesus is good news.

1. **Ready** – Who has some good news to tell us? Who has some bad news?

2. **Set** – Luke 2:4-12. Why is the arrival of this baby such good news? Why is baby Jesus called a Savior, the Messiah (King) and the Lord (Boss)?

3. **Go** – Cabin leader: Tell the story about what happened when you believed the good news about Jesus.

Chapter 7 – You know faith is real when you see it in action.

1. **Ready** – Make a long line on the floor or ground and pretend it's a slackline over hot lava. What tricks can you do on it without "falling" off?

2. **Set** – Proverbs 3:5-6. What does the story about Nabil's mom tell you about what it means to believe in Jesus?

3. **Go** – What do you find hard to believe about Jesus? What do you find easy to believe?

Chapter 8 – Believing in Jesus is harder when you have to.

1. **Ready** – What's something you would enjoy more if you didn't feel like you *had* to do it? What's something you would like to do but it seems too hard?

2. **Set** – Mark 10:17-27 – Why was it so hard for this guy to follow Jesus? Was it impossible?

3. **Go** – What keeps you from following Jesus? What would Jesus ask you to give up?

Chapter 9 – Love for God is not quite the same as love for your family and friends.

1. **Ready** – What do you love? Who do you love? How is love for chocolate ice cream different than love for your family?

2. **Set** – John 15:12-14. Some people are hard to love. Do you think love for God would help you to love people, even the hard ones? Why?

3. **Go** – One of the ways we love people is by forgiving them. This means choosing not to hold something against them anymore. Who do you want to love by forgiving them?

Chapter 10 – We can talk with God like he is really there, because he is.

1. **Ready** – If you had the chance to walk up to God and ask one question, what would it be?

2. **Set** – 1 John 5:14-15. When you ask God for something, how can you tell if it is what he wants for you?

3. **Go** – Find a way that works best for your group to ask God something—out loud, on paper, all praying at the same time, etc.

Chapter 11 – Believing is seeing.

1. **Ready** – Can you think of a movie where someone says, "Seeing isn't believing; believing is seeing?" (Hint: think of two Christmas classics).

2. **Set** – Hebrews 11:3 – Is there anything about the natural world that makes more sense to someone who believes in God?

3. **Go** – Go for a walk (even if it's nighttime) and think/talk about what you see that shows off the amazing craftsmanship of God.

Chapter 12 – We are all on a journey that can lead to faith in Jesus.

1. **Ready** – What's one story about this week that you will tell people at home? Any stories that you would be hesitant to tell them?

2. **Set** – 1 John 2:3-6. How can you tell if you have come to know and love God? What would living like Jesus look like in your own town in the 21st century?

3. **Go** – Practice answering the question people back home will probably ask, "How was camp?" See if you can come up with a better answer than "fine" or "good."

Also by Jim Badke, for leaders:

The Christian Camp Leader

Will you serve at a
Christian camp this
summer? Then this
book is for you!
Prepare your heart,
focus your perspective
and hone your skills as
a camp leader.

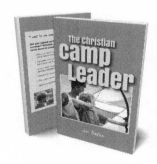

*"The Christian Camp Leader is well-written, accessible
and concise, showing rookies—and reminding veterans—
what camp ministry is all about."* – Bill McCaskell,
One Hope Canada

Jim Badke writes from 40+
years of church and camp
ministry. He and his wife
Sarah and their dog Barkley
live by the lake in
Honeymoon Bay on
Vancouver Island.

---Available on Amazon---
ISBN 978-0-9916846-2-5

Also by Jim Badke, for leaders:

As The Eagle Walks

*If the Apostle John was still
living on the island of
Patmos, would you want to
visit him?*

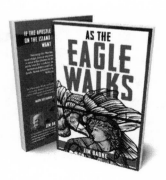

Touring the Mediterranean to save a crumbling
marriage, Jason explores the island of Patmos and
meets a man who claims to be the Apostle John.
Invited to stay with him for a while, Jason wrestles
with the gap he sees between John and his own
understanding of Christian faith. Some Islanders love
this man and others hate him. Will Jason uncover why?

"As The Eagle Walks *pulled me in from its first page
and held me with its richly-drawn characters, vividly-
evoked scenes, crisp and often funny dialogue, and
mounting tension—all the things we look for in a
novel—while exploring real-life matters of faith."*

– Mark Buchanan, author of *God Walk* and *David Rise*

---Available on Amazon---
ISBN 978-1777710101

Manufactured by Amazon.ca
Bolton, ON

33976535R00081